The End of Everything

ALSO BY M. JOHN HARRISON

Novels

Viriconium

Climbers

The Course of the Heart

Signs of Life

Light

Nova Swing

Empty Space

The Sunken Land Begins to Rise Again

Short Story Collections

The Ice Monkey

Things that Never Happen

You Should Come with Me Now

Settling the World

Anti-Memoir

Wish I Was Here

The End of Everything

M. John Harrison

—

First published in Great Britain in 2026 by
Serpent's Tail,
an imprint of Profile Books Ltd
29 Cloth Fair
London
EC1A 7JQ

www.serpentstail.com

3 5 7 9 10 8 6 4 2

Typeset by CC Book Production

Printed and bound in Great Britain by
CPI Group (UK) Ltd, Croydon, CR0 4YY

A CIP catalogue record for this book is available from the British Library.

Our product safety representative in the EU is
BGC Sustainability & Compliance, 7 avenue du Général Leclerc,
Paris, 75014, France https://baldwinglobalconsulting.com

ISBN 978 1 80081 294 9
eISBN 978 1 80081 296 3

FSC www.fsc.org
MIX
Paper | Supporting responsible forestry
FSC® C013604

The End of Everything

PART ONE:

War in Heaven

Tidelines

—

FOR YEARS PHILLIP TENNENT LIVED at the edge of the sea, where artefacts were washed up every day. Scavengers, professional and otherwise, came and went. Turnover was higher than you'd expect given the relaxed lifestyle, the constant good weather, the ease with which some sort of existence could be pursued.

Most of the beachcombers took away the first item they could easily carry and sold it on elsewhere. If you had contacts in the hinterland, there was no doubt about how slickly that could be done. But the hard core like Tennent hung on, out there dawn and dusk, shine or shine, throwing the small ones back, waiting for an item that would give them pause for thought. They were committed. They could be seen from orbit. Their living structures glowed at night a hundred miles up and down the coast. By day you saw that temporary qualities had defined over the decades a permanent aesthetic: bothies and benders made of whitened sticks; mirrors and bits of rag; almost anything the tide left, although to incorporate an artefact would have been considered bad taste as much as bad luck. The beachcombers had their limits. Their superstitions gave the tideline its social structures and distinctive quality on the palate.

Further back from the shore, the hinterland was dark, a little more threatening, with its flattened hashmark of streets and its differing sets of rules. There was a lot of poured cement and half-functioning neon, a lot of territoriality; you had to talk your way through the bars, blockhouses and abandoned car parks to get your item out to market.

Coming up from the intertidal, out of the dusty salt wind with his latest find under one arm, Tennent met a woman on her way down. She looked at the object – which was at that time about the size of a baby, and which he had wrapped in some bleached-out rags – and nodded with a kind of measured approval. They studied the horizon together for a moment, and she asked him what condition the sea was in down there that day.

'Eventually it'll turn into speech,' Tennent said, without knowing why.

They both laughed.

She was carrying a week's groceries in a bag for life with

a broken handle. No one was eating much down there. He thought he'd seen her before, living mostly on her own in a hut a hundred or so metres south of his.

'I'm off,' he said. 'Take anything you want of mine. If you need anything, it's yours.'

Loose white sand blew into the air and whirled around at the edge of the sea like a fog. They turned to face it with similar body language – expectant, alert, anxiety tempered with what could only be described as longing. For a moment Tennent had a sense that something huge was approaching over the water; something fast, which hadn't been there – or indeed anywhere – a minute or two before. But it never arrived, and the woman shrugged.

'You'll be back,' she predicted.

'No, I won't.'

They laughed again and she walked away towards the tide across the perfect sand, the sound her feet made reminding him suddenly of the sound of feet on snow. She waved without looking back.

A house on the borderland

—

THE STRIP WAS ANOTHER KIND of tideline, facing both the ocean and the dry land, the way they always do.

Tennent had a relative there, an aunt of his called Marnie, a painter who occupied an old terraced townhouse on an elbow of raised ground at the outer edge of the town, where the cross streets turned to dirt tracks and fused themselves into the dissected chalk plateau inland. By day, you could look out to sea from the top floor of the house, or, landward, across the curve of a narrow little estuary, at mudbanks, a bridge, an island, levels of water according to the state of the tide, and on the far bank, ruderal scrub from which emerged the remains of buildings. At night, you chose between the faltering neon messages of the Strip, or, in the other direction, darkness.

Marnie had washed up there from London a generation ago, when the Strip was still a thriving arts community, before the crashed airliner raised its buckled starboard wing like a temporary modernist shelter across the gardens on the other side of the road. Seventy years old now, still in some way the repository of Tennent's adolescence and the social structures which had supported it, she seemed lively and determined one minute, precarious the next. Fragility had set in behind the skin of her cheekbones, but she still made art. Her eyes remained clear and she retained an unimpatient sense of her own worth.

'It's sad to think,' he remembered her saying when he was seventeen or eighteen, 'that people have stopped making full use of you as a human being. You feel as if you've let them down by somehow not being persuasive enough.'

Now she stood stiffly at the door and for a moment it seemed to Tennent as if she might not invite him in.

'What's that you have with you?' she said.

In the confusion following the arrival of the iGhetti, he had found his way to her along the coast as if blindfold, relying on some internal compass of nostalgia. As they emerged from the months of collective trauma that blunted the country's understanding of what had happened, unsure where – or perhaps even who – they were, the two of them had been able to do little but sit and talk. It had been a comfort to rehearse their memories of his childhood holidays in Marnie's house when the world was still good, still intact – 'Still blown,' as she had put it, 'like a stream of bubbles, by all that money.' But in the years since he went to live on the tideline, things had changed between them. For him, the house's value lay in its proximity to the sea, and in its basement – essentially a garage, with good lighting and an inspection pit – which connected to the coast road along a short steep concrete ramp. He kept some of his belongings there, and called in only rarely to check on their condition.

'It's nothing,' he said. 'It's just something I picked up.'

'But now it's in my house.'

'You haven't even seen it,' he said. 'All you've seen is a pile of rags.'

'We agreed you wouldn't bring anything here. It's more than what you see: it's growing. It's grown in the minutes you've been standing at my door wondering whether to knock.' They stared at one another, both rendered uncertain by the strength of her feelings. Eventually she stood away to let him enter, adding: 'I never go near the sea. I know what you do down there.'

'It's just some kind of flotsam,' Tennent reassured her. 'Or is it jetsam? I can never remember which is which, can you?'

'You're not a teenager any more, Phillip.'

Later, she gave him baked beans on toast. Squalls swung in across the north bank and obscured the river. They sat looking out of the window, listening to the rain and talking in low voices. Evening came on; behind the remains of the summer house, the tide could be heard rushing up the estuary. The artefact lay under its wraps in a corner, shifting occasionally as they talked. Every so often, Marnie glanced at it and shuddered, but after a while, appearing to lose interest, she closed her eyes and fell silent. Tennent got to his feet.

'I'm just going down to the garage,' he said.

At that, she clutched his arm. 'One of the things I find myself thinking about,' she whispered, 'is how wonderful it would be to fly.'

He stared down at her. He wasn't sure if she was actually awake.

'This morning,' she went on, 'my kitchen doorway was crawling with ants. A bird came in to eat them. It was – what? – one of those little birds with a red breast. Such an opportunist!' The creature had whirred in and out of the kitchen all morning, she said, making itself quite at home. It was on the doormat, on the refrigerator, on the back of a chair, cocking its dark little eye sidewise at everything. 'Sharp as its own beak! Now, tell me: what kind of bird is that?' Memory loss was both a curse and a blessing to her. Sometimes she offered it with a smile – not as an explanation but as a habitation, the place she was speaking from – at others, it simply left her impatient.

'A robin, Marnie. You've always had robins in the garden.'

She nodded thoughtfully; then, after a pause, said in a completely different tone of voice: 'I have my own problems,

Phillip. I've had to work quite hard to keep this place. I've sometimes had to be tougher than I wanted.'

Down in the garage he pulled the dust cover off the bonnet of the vehicle he kept there. Its patchy, matt grey bodywork absorbed the strip light and didn't give much back. Everything still seemed dry and good. Tennent smiled. He fetched the escape kit he kept in a tarpaulin duffle under some carefully curated rubbish in the corner; while he was stowing the bag in the boot of the car, he thought he heard the front door open. 'Marnie?' he called. 'Marnie!' When no answer came, he went back up into the house to collect the artefact. 'Marnie? I'm going now.'

He thought she had fallen asleep again, but she was waiting for him in the hall by the front door. The door hung open. Damp night air was blowing in.

'I set it free,' she said. 'It didn't want to stay and – Phillip? – I didn't want it here.'

'Christ!' said Tennent. 'Free? What are you talking about?' And when she looked away from him: 'Which direction did it go? Did you see?'

She shrugged. 'I know what you're doing down there.'

She wouldn't say what she meant by that, and he returned to the basement, where he got into the car and started it. It wasn't until much later that he discovered that the tarpaulin bag had been opened since his last visit, and one of his pistols was missing.

Marnie dreams of a holiday

—

MARNIE, WHO, BEFORE PHILLIP ARRIVED, had been in the kitchen eating cold porridge without sugar to save her teeth, took up the bowl again and sat at the window. She watched him back the car angrily up the ramp and out on to the empty street, revving the engine then taking his foot off the pedal so that the turbo anti-lag rattled and banged and flared orange in the twilight. He had never been very patient, always unsure what direction to go in.

Later, she slept restlessly, and woke thinking that her doorbell had been ringing. Someone had been calling out too: ringing the bell and calling out. Marnie was so convinced of this she went and opened the front door. Nothing for a moment but the smell of the Strip – salt, fuel oil, rubbish – and the distant sound of the tide. The street was empty. Then a fox began barking in the garden at the rear of the house – three syllables, a pause, three syllables, a pause – and she realised that's what she'd been hearing all along. It was so simple and so eerie.

She got back into bed, pulled the covers up and thought, I'm old and my nerves are bad. My nerves are bad. I'm old and my nerves are bad, until she went back to sleep.

Had something come and gone, some blip, some glitch in things? Had something passed right through her, a whole lifetime or universe, disguised as her neighbour, a bell and a fox? Since the crisis, everyone's life was full of moments like these. It had been a long time since anyone could make sense of anything. She was glad of Phillip's pistol, which she took everywhere in her shopping bag. She hadn't expected to see him again, and she hadn't liked the way the artefact lay under its wraps, or the way, when she released it outside her front door, it had learned to crawl so quickly and made its way so confidently off along the street. It was a good deal bigger than it had been when it came into the house.

I didn't want that thing in here, she told herself. I didn't like anything about it. And then, later: You can't waste food just because it's gone cold.

Perhaps fifty years before the crisis, someone had added a two-storey, two-room wooden extension on to the back of the house. By now it needed repair. It was uninsulated and creaked alarmingly in offshore winds. Marnie used the lower room to store her work, but in the summer she slept in the upper one, which had a good-sized balcony that benefitted from the early light. Next morning, still a little slow from the night's insomnia, she lay out there trying to catch the last of the sun before the shadows moved round. She had been dozing for half an hour when she was disturbed by something falling on her, some kind of liquid, a few drops at first, then a sudden steady splatter. It smelled like urine. When she opened her eyes, she saw, a few feet above her, tottering on the edge of the extension roof, weird and foreshortened, one of the Baker twins, flies open, penis out.

'Golden shower!' the boy shouted. 'How do you like that? Golden shower!'

He turned to run away and put his foot through the extension roof. Rotten plaster pattered down inside. His left leg dangled into the room beneath, scrabbling for purchase. He began to call out in a high voice.

'I have you now, you little bastard,' Marnie told him.

She wiped herself off and went inside, where she rummaged about in the kitchen until she found a metre or two of old electrical flex. This she fastened round the boy's ankle, anchoring the other end to the heaviest object she could find, which happened to be the bed, to limit the movement of the leg. Once she was satisfied, she went outside again and pulled herself up on the edge of the extension roof until she could look at him.

'How do you feel about this now?' she said.

The boy was in a half-sitting, half-kneeling position, his visible leg quivering with the strain of supporting him.

'Hey,' he said. 'My fucking knackers are trapped.' He was about fourteen, with no talent for anything, and up to this moment too big to control. Marnie went back inside. After some consideration, she grasped the tethered leg in both hands and hung from it.

'No one in this street likes you,' she shouted. 'Do you hear?'

Then she found a knife in a cupboard, cut into the boy's femoral artery and stepped quickly away from the spray of blood. She stood there for a moment watching the leg flail and spurt. She went out on to the balcony again. 'What do you say now?' she called. 'Want to piss on someone now?' No answer. She watched for a minute or two as the boy lost energy, then turned away and leaned on the balcony rail, looking up and down the row at the overgrown gardens. The boy was humming sleepily to himself. In his confusion he had taken off his shirt and thrown it on to the balcony. Marnie used it to wipe her stomach again, then dropped it over the rail into the garden and lay back down. She was too late. At this time of year, the airliner's shadow fell across the whole house, tailfin first, and blocked out the sun from eleven o'clock onwards.

'Damn,' she said.

She went and talked to the boy's father, who lived a couple of doors down. They sorted things out between them, and the father sent someone to lever his dead son out of her extension roof.

Rain fell briefly during the next night, to be breathed away by warm air from the southern counties. Marnie dreamed of a holiday she had once spent walking in the Alpes-Maritimes, and the next morning made her way carefully up the long, easy slope of the airliner's unbroken starboard wing, from the highest point of which she could stare out north and east into the bright grey light. There was nothing new. Across the river she thought she could detect faint smudges of smoke from artillery airbursts above the north edge of the Weald. Attack helicopters went to and fro at the limits of vision, nose down against the cloud base.

Closer to, someone was at work on one of the houses at the end of the street. Rubble had been cleared from around its base, scaffolding erected. From a pulley at the top stage of the scaffold, a thick, Victorian-looking rope swung in the wind. Figures were already at work, propping up the bulging facade with timber, putting in rolled steel joists to replace broken lintels. The house looked exhausted. There was no one to live in it anyway. Building projects like these had been a defining feature of the late phases of the crisis, evidence of an aimless energy, the rush to be active that achieves nothing but can't be argued against. All projects, the iGhetti believe, are inherently good. They are good because they are projects.

Later, her neighbour Giovana, who had taught baroque violin before the world changed, and still sometimes spent an hour or two working with the more difficult elements of the chaconne from *Partita No. 2 in D minor*, came to the front door wondering if Marnie had heard noises in the night. Marnie said she had.

'It's the foxes,' she said. 'Would you like breakfast?'

Giovana looked past her into the house. For a moment she seemed to be lost for something to say. Then she shook her head.

'Not while you continue to misappropriate yourself like this,' she said.

At three in the morning, admitting finally that she couldn't sleep, Marnie had descended to the garden, retrieved the dead boy's shirt, and stuck it to her hallway wall with the last of a tube of superglue. Underneath it she had written, 'When you take your clothes to the laundrette, you are reaffirming or celebrating your identity. Some of its components, at least, dance, spin, enumerate themselves in front of your eyes. You are able to renew your acquaintance with them. The distinctive kinds of wear and tear your personality is prone to become apparent – fading, fraying, a loss of colour.' Versions of this conceit, written and rewritten, had expanded to cover most of the wall.

After breakfast the boy's father called, with a delegation comprised of half a dozen other people who lived along the street. 'Some of us feel you went too far,' he said, implying perhaps that he didn't.

One of the women – she was a Norwegian, whose name sounded something like 'Seattle' – pushed in front of him and added: 'He was only twelve.'

Marnie could see the justice of that.

'I thought he was older,' she said. 'Would anyone like some instant coffee?'

'Thanks,' the woman said contemptuously. 'But I never do.'

The general feeling, the father said, the feeling of everyone there, was that Marnie should leave.

'I can see why you might say that,' she said, although she couldn't. She stared along the street trying to remember how long she had lived there before the crisis changed everything, then up at the tailfin of the airliner in the grainy light. Generally, she spent the hour after breakfast reading, or vacuuming the carpets. 'I've lived here longer than any of you, but I can see why you might say that.'

'He was only twelve,' the woman repeated.

Limit case

—

As soon as they left her alone, Marnie went out to shop. Bread was hard to find after nine o'clock. In response, everyone was making their own, buying up all the flour, with the result that, week on week, it became harder still.

After their quarrel, she assumed, Phillip would have driven back to the beach, where even as a teenager he had found it easier to control his fits of temper. While she was at the Strip, she decided, it wouldn't hurt to break with her habit, go down to the tideline, and see if she could find him. She made her way through the dusty car parks, between the deserted gyms and the low, bunker-like concrete structures of the pawnbrokers and artefact-assayers with their steel-shuttered doors and windows. Music blared out of the bars as if there were still holidaymakers on the Strip. Indeed, in the parallelogram of side streets known as Dalston-on-Sea, there may well have been puzzled long-weekenders down from the London enclaves, where, drifting in patches like a kind of weak metaphysical fog, the disaster had failed as yet to make headway. What these academics and middle-scale arts entrepreneurs expected to find, as they ushered their families past the endless trays of common artefacts mudlarked from the intertidal zone, was difficult to guess.

Marnie sat down outside one of the bars, where daily they arranged a cluster of Italianate metal tables among the sea-kale colonies at the top of the storm beach, and asked for a cup of chocolate. The tables were filmed with a coarse whitish powder blown out of the interior on the previous night's off-shore winds. As soon as she sat down, two men arrived and took the very next table to hers.

It was already hot in the bay. A crowd of local children scoured the shingle, restless, unassuaged as gulls, shouting and grunting, uprooting clumps of chamomile and yellow horned poppy and throwing them at one another for something to do. There was a faint compound smell – fish and salt, perfume and fried food. For a moment it seemed like a language, with a shifting, impermanent syntax: but when she listened it had nothing to say. Further out, the beachcombers, fatigued and lethargic-looking, hunched against the wind and shuffled between their wilfully graceless shelters. Mirrors and wind chimes flickered and swung.

The chocolate, when it came, tasted of something else, she couldn't say what. One of the men watched her pulling pieces off the sourdough and dipping them in her cup, and after a moment said:

'Do you always eat like that?'

'Teeth,' Marnie said loudly, opening her mouth to show him. 'Teeth.' When he failed to respond, she pointed at the beach. 'I hate the way these people live, don't you? It's so infantile.' Then confided: 'I came down here to find my nephew, but I haven't seen him or his special car.'

He stared at her for a moment longer, then turned to his companion, who murmured something and laughed.

They were both wearing silk suits without shirts, drinking soft drinks the colour of fruit in an advertisement two generations old. She couldn't place them well enough to understand what they were talking about. She opened her mouth again and made energetic chewing motions. After that, they got up and moved to a table further away, and the rest of their conversation became even more garbled. She thought she heard one of them spell out the word 'toes', then recite, 'House. Louse. Mouse. Yes, mouth. But *touch*.'

Meanwhile, the children had stopped shouting and were looking intently at the water. A hundred yards out, where the shallows fell away and the light hardened up, the sea shone like metal. Just beneath the surface there – so that it appeared as a system of wind-driven ripples in the flicker and dazzle

– something was racing towards the shore. It might have been an object or an animal, it might have been some change in the medium itself. Whatever was happening, a corresponding ripple of motion took place along the beach: soon everyone except Marnie was on their feet, shading their eyes, pointing at the water.

'It won't *be* anything,' she informed the people nearest her. 'It never is.' She licked her finger, dipped it into the substance on the table and took it to her tongue. It was flour. 'I've been coming here all my life,' she added.

She remembered mornings when everything was like high-definition TV, wrapped in the documentary sublime. No horizon line. Distant objects – hikers on the cliffs, seabirds on the harbour mole – seemed too large. Light, silhouettes, perfect saturated colour, all at once. In those days, her paintings had been quite the opposite, barely processed or so she believed, domestic interiors and still lifes of all the traditional subjects. 'Whole worlds,' she had once written to her brother, Phillip's father, 'trapped in a few daisies, some grapes in a bowl.' In those days, she had done out everything in the feathery greys of degreased paint, which made any object look tranquil but also raw and deliberately unfinished – unseen or as-yet-unseen, and yet as if a kind of indoor weathering had taken place on every surface.

'In those days,' she felt bound to tell the people staring out to sea, 'Anne Redpath was my model.'

Easy jets

—

LATE AFTERNOON. A HYBRID SMELL on the wind, like hyacinth and eucalyptus, as Marnie returned home. Children skateboarding in the street stopped to watch an old bomber descending towards London, its variable-plan wing enamelled briefly by the strong light.

Her neighbours, she found, had developed further thoughts about the Baker boy's death: Giovana was addressing them from the front doorstep of the house, keeping her dressing gown carefully closed with one hand. In the other she held by the neck one of her favourite violins, a Thomas Smith circa 1768 with its original boxwood pegs intact. This she displayed as if she were thinking of performing for them, or as if the violin were in itself an explanation of something. In the face of such complex body language, they seemed, for the moment, uncertain.

Before any of them could catch sight of her, Marnie made her way quietly out of the street, pushed through some rotten garden fences and climbed on to the asbestos roof of a neighbouring garage. From there, obscure in the deep shadow of the crashed airliner's tailfin, she could keep an eye on the situation while she decided what to do.

Some people missed one thing from the pre-disaster world, some people another. Everyone had their favourite. Marnie missed air travel. Where she couldn't remember people's names, and facts often confused her, she still had a good memory for every flight she had ever made. The orange and white tailfin belonged to an Airbus A330-200 which, before the disaster brought it down, had daily navigated the trade routes between Heathrow and Mediterranean Europe. On its upper wing, she knew, she would be able to find two small, solid-looking eye bolts painted a refreshing yellow: staring out of the window during a holiday flight, short or long haul, she had always been reassured by those bolts, although she had no idea what they were for.

The only thing she hadn't liked about air travel was the food. Something about the smell of it in the confined fuselage, she thought, often made you feel sick. That was before you ate it. The smell would saturate the cabin via the air conditioning, half like food, half like some kind of dishwasher residue, while on the tiny screens above the seats, James Bond made silent grimaces intended to convey irony, puzzlement or pleasure.

But Marnie thought she would be willing, like most people, to forgive all that now, and take the jet once more to the vanished havens of Zakynthos, Mexico, Sri Lanka.

Outside her house the argument continued. There was some shouting, but Marnie could make sense of nothing except her own name, and for a minute or two this caused her to feel she no longer existed except as a story people were telling each other. By now, Giovana had retreated a step or two into the hall, from which position she seemed to be trying to explain Marnie's collage of the night before. She reached up abruptly and pulled the boy's shirt from the wall, as if to emphasise some critical point. Marnie, seeing that the situation would remain unresolved unless she made some contribution, stood up and shouted, 'Hey!' Once she was certain she had their attention, she took the pistol out of her shopping bag and began firing. At that range – it was nearly a hundred yards – she didn't expect to hit anything, but two of them fell down. The others first milled helplessly about, then, unsure perhaps whether they were running away from the shots or towards Giovana, surged up the front steps and into Marnie's house. The violinist was knocked over and trodden underfoot along with her instrument. Quite clearly above the sounds of shouting, Marnie heard the Thomas Smith's final plangent chord.

She waited until it had died away, put the pistol back in her shopping bag and ran off down the road, full of an energy she didn't yet understand. Before she left the house that morning, in case Tennent returned before her, she had written him this note –

'My problem has always been that I couldn't quite believe that groups of people could be so predictably crass. Who knows what we've done to one another here. Before the disaster or since, it's been one tainted project after another. We're all exhausted from trying to find the thin slice of territory we don't affect, somewhere that will allow us to occupy it without leaving an impression.' She wasn't quite sure what she meant by this, except that all anyone wanted to know was, had they drawn the iGhetti to Earth? 'It's always seemed important to know if we're their victims or our own.' Then: 'You will look after yourself, won't you?' And, finally, addressing herself, perhaps, rather than Phillip: 'Age is an immense sadness that seems to be folded into everything.'

What were the iGhetti and where had they come from?

They had seemed at first like neither a thing nor a picture of a thing: they seemed to be extruded from a space that wasn't quite in the world. Various simple beliefs surrounded the invasion. Competing authorities associated the iGhetti with dark matter or with the banking crisis of the late 2000s, while others believed it to be less an invasion than a 're-enchantment of the world', a process of spiritual tourism and gentrification pursued by advanced civilisations from a mooted ninth planet. More popularly, they were seen as having 'come out of the internet': indeed, this was the favoured theory of the internet itself; the medium still firmly – if a little desperately – casting itself as the message.

While none of these explanations could be described as true, they did, perhaps, mirror the type and scale of the anxieties that led the iGhetti to us. The truth was simpler. They had leaked into our world long before, from the astral plane. Originally, most of them were found dead. At first they could manifest only as a kind of transparent jelly that was not to be confused with ectoplasm. It was to be found spread on grass and the trunks of trees. In this form, for hundreds of years, the iGhetti were known as 'astromyxin' or 'astral jelly'. Then, quite suddenly, at the turn of the 1980s, their efforts became both more determined and more successful.

The new form appeared only in West London and only near water, its appearance being passed off as a pollution issue. A sophisticated hydrogel was hypothesised, emergent from unknown processes taking place deep in the waste dumps and abandoned settling basins of the cosmetic and regenerative medicine industries. It had learned to mimic the behaviour of living systems, acquiring memory as part of a rapid development of complex adaptive behaviours. Further research eliminated the possibility. In any case, it soon became clear that this was only an intermediate stage of the organism – if it could be said to be one. No one knew what form a mature specimen might take. Lakes and reservoirs were their preferred location, but they were also found on the banks of streams, and on one occasion at the edge of the carp pool in the Temperate House at Kew Gardens. Soon they had rolled down the river from Richmond to Chelsea, and thence to the City of London, which they promptly infested, appearing as tall writhing bursts of light above the skyline, often at evening. Were they 'here', in any sense a human being could understand?

That was it for some years. Although their influence spread from primary nodes in New York, Dubai and especially the great Chinese banking cities, in London the iGhetti seemed content to be contained by the Square Mile. You had the sense they were focussed on other projects. New buildings began to appear, for instance – elaborate, not entirely stable parodies of 00s vanity architecture, which lasted a week or a month before toppling slowly away into a kind of dark blue air. For Londoners, things went downhill during that time. The sirens would go off, all across the city from Borough to Camden. The artillery would fire and recoil, fire and recoil. Our bombers would sweep in. The iGhetti would pulse and grow against the lighted clouds. Who knew if what happened then could be described as 'retaliation'? They were gone again for another day, another week, another month, leaving behind a different world. Life's grain had suddenly become both knotted and indistinct. Events which had previously flowed in a dependable stream became sketchy and indeterminate. Were these distortions a weapon in themselves, or only a side issue of the iGhetti's way of existing? Whether a person could rescue anything from their individual circumstances would now depend very much on how determined they could be, on what they could ignore. It was a different kind of existence.

None of this made any sense to Marnie. In that, she shared the situation of around eight billion other human beings on the planet.

A bad patch

—

Use of this term was as problematic as the crisis itself.

People often described the City of London as 'the bad patch', the most noticeable, most permanent evidence that things had gone wrong. But they would also describe a change in their local reality as a bad patch as if it were a basically economic fluctuation, reducing the value of their houses or the social capital concentrated on their bookshelves or in the art on their walls. 'The country's going through a bad patch,' they might say. Or: 'We're coming out of a bad patch in our lives.' Using the phrase in its older, pre-crisis sense – the way you might talk about a failed marriage or career – was perhaps an unconscious attempt to normalise the inexplicable and minimise the disaster.

Static phenomena were all over London by then, permanent

features of a street, or even a corner of someone's house, while smaller, unanchored events drifted about like fogs or showers of rain, or perhaps more like temporary shifts of the light on a predominantly sunny day. The middle classes, even if they lived near a bad patch – or had one in their garden, or if their corner shop had disappeared into one – tried to avoid mentioning it.

Phillip Tennent had experienced his first bad patch at ten or eleven years old, on the Thames footpath at Hammersmith Bridge, as he stood waiting for some other children by the railings of St Paul's school playing field. At that age he was still uncertain about the river and its moods, rendered as anxious by low tide as he was by the silhouettes of the partly foundered boats further upstream at Brent. The previous day, he had watched a heron eating a live eel on the mudbank at the foot of the south pier of the bridge. Now the mud was under water, but the heron still waited. Phillip's friends were late to appear. No one was answering his calls.

Shortly past midday, a dozen military helicopters ground across in front of him, east to west, line astern, heading upriver. Tennent jumped and waved. He dialled a number, pointed his phone into the air and shouted, 'Can you hear this? Wow! Can you hear? Close air support!' He pressed the phone to his ear, then pointed it back at the sky. 'Can you hear? Something's happening!' Groaning and clattering with the effort of it, the machines disappeared towards Oxford.

Tennent's elation soon dispersed. Shortly afterwards, though, a thirteenth helicopter struggled into view, curving low over Hammersmith from the north. It was grey and without identification marks. Its rotors pieced up the air. It was a long way behind the others but didn't seem to be hurrying to catch up. It turned slowly upside down then drifted back towards Chelsea, losing height, while below, the Thames seemed to widen briefly and the atmosphere turned a colour Tennent couldn't describe.

'I knew the pilot was in trouble,' he told his mother. 'I rang everyone but they weren't all that interested. It's not that they were uninterested, they just weren't as interested as me. That was *so frustrating*.'

'I'm sure it was,' his mother said, not unkindly.

Tennent felt he still hadn't got his meaning across. The helicopter – floating rather than flying, turning turtle in its dignified, inevitable way, in brownish air and sudden, complete silence, then descending slowly into the Thames – had filled him with the raw excitement you always feel in early adolescence when you think some family disaster is going to break the monotony, or when the TV announces another war. Things are going to change now, you think. Whatever happens, they'll never be the same again. You can't quite communicate to anyone how different things are going to be. A month later, things are still the same; everyone else is right and you were wrong.

'What I didn't have the heart to tell you at the time,' his mother would reveal much later, 'was that when people were standing there, they often saw the same crash. Not always, not everyone. But often it's what they saw.'

Nine grammes

—

FOR WANT OF ANY OTHER idea, and assuming that the artefact would try to make its way back to the sea, Tennent had taken the coast roads after he left Marnie's house.

At first, he drove in a rage, too fast and in the wrong direction, away from the Strip and out into the nowhere of the old customs zone, where the chains of abandoned container yards, shining from a week's rain, stretched north and east like shallow lakes towards Dover. The roads were empty everywhere. Above him the night was crawling with new constellations. In front, the tarmac turned up town after town of cheap low-rise dormitories, which had served a pre-disaster population of border patrol workers, all deserted now, their haloed traffic lights red, red and red against him in the thin Channel mist.

Every two or three miles, Tennent found his progress halted by an apparently functionless roadblock, each upgraded Newey barrier attended by a maze of low concrete walls, backed up by an ICV or two, and staffed by men in the unbadged and unrecognisable uniforms of competing authorities. Members of militias or special forces, they were experienced, heavily armed and bored. Their body language implied that they were used to better. With the coming of the iGhetti, the military apparatus of the state had regained all its sense of entitlement, while the City of London, puzzled and defeated, had relinquished the top spot in the conversation and could only huddle at the edges of its old power base, like a monarchist staring into a museum display.

By the time Tennent had recognised his mistake and been turned aside by the last of the roadblocks, it was two in the morning. He found the Strip cold and empty. An onshore wind blew waste paper across the parking area. He got out of the car and walked about until he heard shouts and laughter echoing nearby. Five or six men stood around under a streetlight, shouting and laughing at something in the road. Every so often one of them dodged forward and kicked at it. It lay there laughing feebly up at him. By now it had the size, if not quite the shape, of a ten-year-old child, with smooth facial features and wisps of hair on a round, predominantly bald skull. Its blue eyes shone in the streetlight. Neither frightened nor puzzled, it looked as if it was living somewhere else; as if it hadn't quite contacted the world in which it found itself. Even the men could see that, and were stirred to a kind of outrage as a result. They had a curious grace as they skipped forward, shoulders hunched, hands in pockets, to deliver a kick. Tennent decided he could deal with them, but not all at once. He watched for a moment or two as they worked themselves up towards the inevitable climax, then slipped away into one of the empty buildings, where he lay quietly down on a bed, pulled the collar of his jacket up round his neck and went to sleep.

When he woke it was still dark.

Out in the street they had made quite a big fire and had begun cutting up the artefact. It was still moving its arms and legs listlessly, but its flesh was coming off in thin slices, translucent as sandwich ham in the firelight. They had already removed one of its hands. As soon as they began to eat the flesh, it made them drowsy. Tennent took out his gun and went round shooting them in the base of the skull. 'Nine grammes for you,' he said. 'And nine for you, too.' He got his hands under the artefact's primitive arms and hauled it to his car, where he tried to make it comfortable. It was hybrid technology, some kind of biological gadget the iGhetti had released in numbers when they first arrived, which was no longer of use to them. It stared up at him from a pale, lopsided face and made wavery motions with its arms. The missing hand had already begun to regenerate.

It looked like a puddingy lump, but it was developing as you watched.

'Hello, nice,' it said.

'Don't try to talk,' Tennent advised it from the driver's seat.

He stared out into the dark all night. Just before dawn there was some activity among the beachcombers – shouts, high-lumen torches sweeping the tideline – then brief oily lozenges of colour on the surface of the water further out.

The things she had in her bag

—

MARNIE SAT BESIDE THE COAST road, staring vaguely around. She wondered for a moment where she was and how she had got there, then remembered. Evening was on its way. Goodness, she thought. I'd better do something. The wind had turned and the weather with it. A fine rain was blowing out to sea as if it had news from the land.

Since that morning, she hadn't known what to make of herself; the day had been full of elation one minute, loneliness the next. She was used to a bad memory, but less used to being so uncertain about things in general. Anxiety overcame her at the thought, and this caused her to ransack her belongings in their cotton tote. Her purse was clearly lost, then she found it, as you always do, right at the bottom of the bag. Down there too the pistol lay, heavy, black, convincing, wrapped in socks;

and beneath that a sediment of tiny gold-leaf snowflakes, relic of some distant Christmas.

She picked up the pistol, smelled it. Held it near her head then quickly replaced it and covered it over.

Everything's changed, she thought. I'll never go home now. Not now. In some ways it was a relief.

Just then a figure came striding briskly along the road from the direction of the Strip. At first it was only a silhouette, a sense of motion against the lights. Closer to, it turned into a woman in her late forties, tall, with a ropy muscularity, dressed in a sleeveless top – partnered with neo-Celtic tattoos, men's athletic shorts, orange knee-length compression socks and brown leather hiking boots – and talking quite loudly into a smartphone. 'Yes, I do,' she said. 'But the lasagne's not such good quality.' Coming abreast of Marnie – apathetically squatting at the kerb surrounded by her collection of small belongings – she glanced down without interest and carried on past. 'I know, I know,' she was saying, 'but they didn't get it wrong like that, did they?' Then, 'Yes, well, he is. He *is* always calling her out for her posture.'

'I don't know where all the *snowflakes* came from,' Marnie shouted after her, holding up a pinch of them and letting them fall. 'Or what they were for!' She laughed. 'Sorry to be in your way.'

The woman went on a little further without acknowledging these overtures, then turned back suddenly.

‘Excuse me?’ she said.

‘Oh nothing,’ said Marnie.

‘Only I thought you might have implied something about my dog,’ the woman said. ‘People often do. They’re offended by him for reasons not entirely clear. His name is Andrew. He’s quite big. He’s a cross-breed, but they don’t realise that.’

Marnie said she didn’t know anything about dogs.

‘They think he’s a Basuto.’

‘Now, there, you see. I thought a Basuto was a kind of pony. That was the impression I had.’

At this the woman only looked puzzled and admitted: ‘I’ve lost him.’

‘I’d help you look,’ Marnie offered, ‘if I could just get everything back in this bag.’ They walked about between the shingle and the old seafront mansions, calling the dog’s name. Once or twice, Marnie thought she saw something lolloping about, in and out of some bushes a little way further on. It was, she thought, a sort of greyish white. But apparently you could expect even a Basuto cross to be quite a lot darker than that – really another colour altogether, which the woman said she would have trouble describing, particularly in the twilight. ‘He won’t come back,’ she kept reporting into the smartphone. ‘He’s not coming back this time.’ She was right. If there had been a dog at all, it didn’t come back and eventually she seemed to lose interest and wandered off. Marnie, now committed, cried out the animal’s name again, as loud as she could, drawing out the second syllable. 'Andrew! Andrew!' At that, a hundred gulls wheeled up from a line of granite boulders imported to protect the promenade from the year-on-year migration of the shingle, and her desolate mood returned.

In the gathering dark, the beach looked normal. The sea, too, though a flat track of moonlight lay on its surface, parallel to the beach and about five hundred yards out, sometimes swelling and broadening in an oily fashion as if some large object had suddenly changed course beneath. She trudged down to Phillip's bothy, the only patch of darkness in a row of yellow lamps and fires just above the tideline, but found it deserted. She hadn't really expected anything else. Music and laughter rose from closer to the water. There were lively smells of cooking. Welcome to the liquid world, she told herself.

Strings of solar-powered garden lights came on feebly as she entered the bothy, revealing a structure of whitened driftwood smooth and hard as bone, woven into the ad hoc lattices and tangles of an approximate dome. There was a floor of wooden pallets, at the centre of which Phillip had pitched a small tent. Everything else was disordered. None of it was worth much. Someone might have got use out of the laptop or the single burner stove. Otherwise, it was MDF shelves tacked together awkwardly with nails too large; corroded engine parts; a small laminated-ply tabletop propped up on bricks. Half-burnt novelty candles adhered to every surface. Lengths of braided orange and blue polypropylene hung from high in the ceiling, unravelling in the draughts. Among beachcombers, a serious item from the ocean was often referred to as a ticket, she knew: your ticket out. The moment he thought he had secured his, Phillip had abandoned everything he owned. They all did it. It was a point of honour, a kind of diffusion or moral distribution of yourself into the general project, via the things you would no longer need. It was the closest form of behaviour they had to a politics.

Turning this stuff over calmly in the undependable light, Marnie opened a damp-fattened paperback book, only to read, 'What happens to you the first time you wonder whose life you're looking at? It's not your own, but it isn't anyone else's either,' and close again it briskly. She gave some time to a framed photograph of the young woman who had come south with Phillip all those years ago; then to their tent, which contained a double sleeping bag and mat laid out neatly with a rechargeable lantern at the head. Inside the sleeping bag a faint, unlikely smell of perfume seemed to linger, but otherwise things seemed clean and tidy enough. Then, tucked down inside, she found a sheaf of papers, curled and yellowed, fastened together with a bulldog clip attached to a short loop of ribbon. They proved to be years' worth of email transcripts, Marnie's to him.

On his eighth birthday, she had begun: 'Darling Phillip, I don't suppose you'll be old enough to understand this.'

What in retrospect seemed like an extraordinary, almost comical failure to find a voice suited to him – or, for that matter, herself – continued through the period that came to be called the iGhetti Summer and across the following half decade, into the months during which he had struggled down the coast from London through the late mayhem of the invasion. In the years since then, the bulldog clip had rusted; sun and salt had bleached the ribbon unevenly from maroon to the faintest pink. The text had faded on the page. What might have happened to Phillip wasn't so clear. We were all of us, at least in the beginning, Marnie thought, thrust back inside ourselves by circumstance. Back into the refuge of our humanity because we thought we could now be certain there was something outside it; something which, though it was here now, fully extant and recognisable, might not entirely understand that we were here too. The contemporary fear was that we might have brought all this – whatever it was – on ourselves.

In the end, her memory would index most of that period by the weather. One year by its constant drizzle, the next by early magnolia in a West London street. Phillip's mother threw a handful of petals in the sunny air and laughed, complaining: 'He's so serious for an eight-year-old!' Conversations with either of them had seemed so uneven, even then. She left the bothy and went outside to pee.

The air was cold, the moon had risen; by its light she imagined for a moment she could see a shoal of small objects moving hopefully towards the beach. She shivered, hurried back inside, struggled into the sleeping bag and fell asleep with her clothes on.

Dear Phillip –

—

– DO GIVE SOME TIME to the enclosed!

Everything in the picture has been driven mad by the light. Do you see? The ocean, the beach, the people, the objects. The frozen yet energetic motion of the waves, clouds, bathers, ships, *everything* is an accident of the painted light – a pure 1930s light, from an imagination stocked when people could use words like 'spiritual' and still mean something.

Light and wind, waxy or chalky or degreased. As raw, muted, incomplete, contemporary, infused, trembling on the edge of some disaster of immanence as their vision allowed. I'll never get tired of trying to describe what English art – cooped up between a failing metaphysics, modernism and two world wars – could suggest about the universe by looking at a kitchen or a row of shops. We don't have a language for it these days, do we? Maybe they didn't have it then either and I'm looking at something I've invented.

Oh Phillip, I know you're a bit too young to understand this now, but later I'm sure you'll see what I mean!

– Well of course I wanted to wish you a happy birthday! Of course I did! Eleven is such an important age!

– I dreamed last night I was out looking for someone: I had to go on foot (and here's the strange part of the dream) and I had to take a small bird with me! The person I was looking for could be described like this: a boy, younger than fifteen but quite grown-up: intellectually mature, companionable, at ease with people. Do you know anyone like that? Though I worried that the bird might fly off and get lost, I was looking forward to seeing the boy, whose ideas and ability to talk were already attracting the interest of writers and teachers. But Phillip, do you see what the bird means? Don't, whatever you do, do what I did with my life, and let your cleverness turn you into an observer.

– Darling, I'm not sure I agree, whatever your mother says. For instance, none of us know what happened to the City of London. Is it still there? Are the iGhetti inside? Do we belong to them now? Or do our lives still belong to the City as it used to be?

– How delightful – now you're a 'young adult' I don't even know when you're joking.

– I have to say I can barely remember being twenty and alone in London with my whole life ahead of me! How does it feel? Are you sure you want the job? You must tell me at length. I walked to the top of the cliffs today, so I could look down at the net sheds, the boating lake, the Speed Wave machine in Flamingo Park, the amusement arcade. It was all still there, despite everything that's happened since you and I last went down to play Whac-a-Mole! Nostalgie de la view, but even now that arcade is the perfect miniature of capitalism, every attraction screaming to be heard above the next; every one of them offering something you can't have.

– It's so nice to hear from you. It feels as if we haven't talked for ages. You write, 'All along the Thames, boats are on their way to being islands, islands on their way to being boats.' Then something you overheard on the Embankment, a woman calling to her little girl: 'Don't run!' Then: 'Daphne! No more running! You're going to hurt yourself.' And you add, 'There'll be no more running in Daphne's life, in case she hurts herself. She's three.' When I reread that paragraph of your mail, I experience a weird déjà vu, as if you told me this – or at least something similar to this – described some encounter of the same sort – a long time ago. Of course, you couldn't have, but it's strange, and the whole content of the scene is strange too, I don't know why. Oh Phillip, one thing you should never say is 'You and I go over and over the past too much'.

– Since you left London, enormous trucks have been moving loads of shingle up and down the same mile-long stretch of coast. They're supposed to be building a new border control facility, but it all seems so random. Meanwhile mist gathers and gathers on the horizon to the south, however sunny it is here, moving a fraction closer every day. You say: 'We're suspended in this new catastrophe. We're held in suspension. It's ongoing and unresolved. It never ends. The nature of the catastrophe is that it has no nature. Not for us. It's permanent, but I don't mean that in Walter Benjamin's sense.'

Well, in what sense do you mean? The only other sense seems to be that everything has gone wrong and we all hate it.

– I love the stairs in this house. I cleaned them again this morning. I clean them often, mainly as an excuse to be on them, to be in close contact with them. I love to be abroad on these stairs. I love their proportions, their cool, still air. They have a calmness which easily transmits itself to me. I think I'd live on these stairs if I could! Lock all the doors to the rooms, except the bathroom and the kitchen. Sleep on the top landing, work on the next one down. There'd be plenty of space. And plenty of light coming in through the long windows. I could keep my stuff in a blanket box. I love blanket boxes. I wouldn't own much – a couple of pairs of trousers, underwear. There would just be room for a mattress on one landing, a desk and chair on the other. The outdoor clothes I could hang in the hall, that wouldn't change; shoes I'd line up in the hall, too. I'm not sure whether I'd allow myself to leave the house, but I suppose I'd have to. It's not a matter of dealing with claustrophobia – because how could you suffer claustrophobia in all this space and light? – so much as doing the shopping, or getting exercise. I suppose I could have stuff delivered. If I absolutely had to go out, I'd try to confine myself to the garden as much as possible, and on wet days stare out of the landing windows at the sea in the distance, or the garden hollyhocks bending in the rain. Hollyhocks are ridiculously tall. Strictly speaking, the garden isn't quite where the stairs end. They make another turn and continue down into the cellars.

– It's sunny now, and you can see the lost continent as a line in the distance. It seems so close! But soon the fog will roll in or close down and it will be gone again. No one ever comes back from there to say whether they found it or not. Items continue to wash ashore, without reminding us of anything we once knew. Kneel at the window all you like in the weak, warm sun, nothing will ever be the same again and you will never remember how things were anyway.

– I'm so glad you're nearly here now. Oh darling, it must have been such a trying journey for you. If I'm not in, you'll find the key in the usual place. A ridiculous dream last night, by the way! A young man paddleboarding down a misty river to the sea. It's dawn. His feet bare. A white shirt worn over jeans, the cuffs of both rolled loosely. What at first seems like a narrow estuary – lilies, slow water, pastel pinks and greens – broadens into a calm sea or lake. A huge, slow fish surfaces partially, hardly disturbing the water, and swims along beside him. He leads it back inland. What do you make of that? The next time I saw him, the fish had changed into something else. It all took place in silence and I woke up laughing. Phillip, is this how you're travelling down the coast? Still innocent, still as open to the world as you were at thirteen? In my dream, I must say, you had remarkably beautiful ankles.

Lost species

—

THE REMAINS OF THE OLD ferry terminal had a subduing effect. Its only usable dock now processed the coast's increasingly busy emigration trade. There weren't many buildings left. Everything took place outside, in what had been the lorry parks. Tennent let the car roll down between the windswept lines of anxious middle-class travellers and, where the concrete gave way to shingle, coarse vegetation and heaps of some discarded substance that resembled gigantic burst tyres, turned left and drove for perhaps half a mile to the Gauf brothers' yard. He got out and stood staring at the sea, tilting his head as if he could smell something he couldn't name. It was a cold morning at the breaker's; nothing much had happened overnight, except for a touch of rain on a brisk onshore breeze. At the horizon – which to the eye came and went undependably – the blades of derelict wind turbines turned, faltered, turned again, while every so often, a prolonged, distant wailing noise could be heard rolling across the bay from one of the other yards.

He leaned into the car and told the artefact, 'Stay here. And don't fiddle with your hand like that.'

'I don't want it,' the artefact said. 'I don't want this hand.'

'Well, you've got it now, like it or not.'

He found the Gaufs in a modular building they had borrowed from some abandoned middle school and jacked up on stilts against the late summer tides. Inside, it resembled the office of an upscale minicab company in 1996 – although the Gaufs were proud that they had decided to keep the children's art, pinned haphazardly on the walls – perhaps because its energetic fantasies of media success reflected their own. Originally cultural entrepreneurs from West London, they had come south on the corporate ticket somewhat before the arrival of the iGhetti. You occasionally saw them around the Strip in their silk suits worn without shirts, but they still believed religiously in slim-fit Paul Smith for the office, airforce blue with a black shirt or charcoal with a dark blue shirt, and always a red, satin-looking tie. Breaking was a trade too new to have developed reliable working practices – or even a clear idea of the resources being exploited – maintained off the back of cheap, effectively indentured labour and run by people like them who believed in the 100 per cent transferability of business skills to any other discipline. This gave them a specialised view of the world. No one could even be sure they were brothers, only that it had always been convenient to them to be known that way.

'Hey, it's our beachcomber!' one of them said.

'How's that cottage industry of yours doing?' the other asked. He got up and came round the desk and shook Tennent's hand. 'We support it wherever we can. We think that's important.'

'I've got an item you might want to see,' Tennent said.

'We were on the Strip just yesterday. Coincidentally it was our day off. Give your mother our regards. Lively woman.'

Tennent stared at him.

'She's not my mother,' he said. 'What made you think that?'

After a moment, he added, 'Leave her alone.'

To this they responded with smiles of mixed puzzlement and irony, and no one said anything until Tennent invited them outside to examine the item. Out there they were uncomfortable, looking about, wincing in the cold wind, knocking on the car windows to attract the attention of the artefact, which had gone to sleep again, then dodging back in surprise when it woke up and showed them its face. It seemed startled but pleased to see them; knocked on the window in return.

'You can see what this is,' Tennent said. 'We haven't had anything like it since the early days.'

'Are you even here?' the artefact called.

The Gaufs weren't sure what they thought. They seemed perturbed, and recommended he didn't keep it much longer. 'You're already looking a bit the worse for wear,' one of them warned, then offered, 'We'll give you something for the car. Just for old times' sake. I love these BMWs.'

Tennent stared at him. 'It's a Lancia,' he said.

'We're not all that keen on the colour.'

'It's a 1986 Delta Integrale,' Tennent persisted. 'It's been through a lot of rebuilds since, so I don't what you'd call it now. Someone uprated it to 700 hp for hill-climbing. But listen, it was never a BMW.'

'What we loved were those Art Cars. Do you remember those? We loved the Rauschenberg BMW!'

Tennent laughed. 'You can't afford the car,' he said.

As he spoke, something cut sharply across his vision, less an object than the shadow of one, and he lurched sideways into false memories of himself, out in the shallows in strong sunshine a hundred metres from a much warmer beach, staring back inland at the highline of a recent tide strewn with the yellowish swim bladders of unknown animals, like condoms inflated then varnished into fragility. Rusty tin signs and nests of polypropylene netting bunched in between maroon sandstone boulders. Then cliffs, and an abandoned funicular railway slicing through the sandstone to the plateau above! From the sea-facing edges of that hinterland, the windows of ice cream parlours and chip shops glittered with promise in the light. Someone he couldn't quite make out, whispering, 'The curses attendant on stealing ocean secrets.' Then, 'No one will ever know what this is!' Later Tennent lounged in the stern of the boat, tired and happy, dazzled by the glare off the surface of the sea, washing a delicate blue object in gentle solvents.

When he came out of the fugue, it was to hear a different person advising him, 'You could try Hampson.' It turned out to be one of the Gaufs. When they saw he'd been through a bad patch, they led him back gently to the Portakabin, made him sit down and gave him a small bottle of mineral water, a clean glass and space to recover. After he'd sat for a bit, shaking and looking at the wall, one of them said, 'Though it's interesting, I don't think we're quite comfortable with your item? You should get rid of it soon. Maybe try it with Hampson? That would probably be the best idea.'

'Thanks for nothing,' Tennent said. 'Jesus. Hampson.'

His own voice sounded clotted to him, confined to his skull but at the same time not properly located in his body, as if he was hearing someone else trying to catch his attention from across the room.

When he returned to the car, the artefact was sitting awry but alert in the driver's seat, staring ahead of itself. It had opened one of the windows a crack. All the car's instruments and warning lights were lit up and flickering wildly. Tennent watched for a moment or two, to see if anything else would happen, then reached in and switched off the engine. The lights continued to flicker for a moment, then faded slowly.

'Get in the back,' he said.

The artefact stared up at him. Whatever he asked, it would do.

'So pure,' it said.

For the rest of the journey, it slept fitfully, waking suddenly for no reason, staring excitedly out of the window as if it had seen something it recognised, then losing energy and looking around with a helpless air. Tennent was tired too. In retrospect, the bad patch puzzled him. It had seemed so pointedly aimed at him, yet so personally irrelevant: though it presented as one, it wasn't a memory. Generally, a patch had a more public narrative as well as a more obvious one. It placed you in the position of an accidental spectator. Everyone saw roughly the same thing, as though the world was patiently replaying an extract from its repertoire for an audience that would never quite understand it.

Before he left the breaking yard, the Gauf brothers had taken him aside and advised, 'Really, you should have thrown this one back.' He was beginning to agree. He'd borrowed a phone off them and left messages when Hampson didn't answer.

The artefact began whispering to itself in something that might have been another language. Once, it brought its vaguely delineated face close to the back of his neck and said, 'It's just what I do.' The missing hand continued to regenerate, although it was still like the art object a conscientious child makes from putty. But Hampson! Tennent thought. Hampson was the beachcomber's call of last resort, a man no one liked, or liked to deal with. No one liked what he did with the things they sold him.

Neutral zones, disintegration loops

—

MARNIE WOKE EARLY NEXT MORNING. The weather was still dull, with a fine rain blowing up from the Channel. She decided she would have a swim. But the water proved too cold for that, and it had felt stupid to wince over to the sea in her underwear. So she got dressed again and started walking north instead, leaving the bothy almost as she had found it – first she took the young woman's photograph out on to the shingle, where she carefully broke up the frame with a large flint. Who had promised what to whom, she wondered, in that relationship? She detached the picture from the frame and skimmed it into the sea, where it floated for a minute before it was snatched down by something under the surface.

The Strip and its economic influence thinned out quickly, to be replaced by a geography of tall black net sheds, rusting diesel winches, dilapidated fishing boats and, to landward, a coastal path shared by dog walkers, joggers and cyclists: all watched over by terraces of peeling but self-sufficient Edwardian housing. Every four or five hundred yards, the wind blew strongly from a different quarter, filling her with a kind of transient elation. A blunt white promontory, the beginning of a transition from sandstone to chalk, grew larger each time she looked up. Here you found distinctive curves where sky and sea conjoined above shingle expanses, inexplicable expanses of concrete, and watery expanses shading from muddy green to a mouldy olive or cobalt blue; very distinctive curves where different surfaces met, intersected or obscured one another. Beside the path, by contrast, lines of black railings and memorial benches directed traffic north along a fiercely ruled perspective – ordering it and being ordered by it in an endless reflex of meaning.

Marnie read the names on the benches. *James, Beloved Father, Grandfather and Husband* would no longer stare comfortably into the distance after his lunch. The shell of him had been blown out to sea – leaning forward a little off the vertical, its jacket open in the wind at last, knees slightly bent, heels raised – on and on until it reached the astral plane and a new life. James, she thought, would have had no choice in this. By then he would have shed too much weight. One day he would simply have lost agency in the face of a brisk offshore wind. It would have been resignation, in all senses of the word.

Her hips and ankles being stiff, she rested frequently. As the morning developed, the sun whitened the cloud base from above, then broke through. By midday, the sky was open, blue and urgent, calling forth the retirees from their second-floor mansion flats. For them, nothing had changed. The women smiled into the sun in a kind of secretive delight: this morning they had found themselves, after all, still alive. The beloved grandfathers, soon queuing formally and amicably at the abandoned public toilet, rehearsed for each other their personal historical understandings of the coast: amiable arguments about the exact nature of Henry the Eighth's fortifications – which everyone could admit were never much use – pivoted with barely a pause for breath to the image of bright white contrails, those dogfights across the beautiful cold azure 1940s sky when England's day was saved at its last moment by doomed young men and a 27-litre liquid-cooled V-12 aircraft engine! There was little sense that any of them acknowledged how disconnected from itself – let alone from its crafted headlong self-myth – their world had become, or even if they had noticed at all.

Late in the afternoon they would be replaced by mothers with toddlers. Before this could happen, Marnie retreated to the shingle, a struggle to walk on but valuable for the way it absorbs and isolates the human figure. Toddlers, she believed, are always trying to convey one of two things: that they want something they know you won't give them, or that they don't want to go somewhere you're going. Eventually, they'll be reconciled to the understanding that nothing anyone wants – or doesn't want – fits the fantasy of it anyway. After that, she thought, and leaving aside some other processes, we're all free not to desire anything at all.

By evening, having covered four or five miles, perhaps more, she was worn out. Over the course of the day, the shingle had become steadily less bare – first spotted with curiously uncomfortable-looking clumps of holm oak; then with dense little islands of it, still quite separate but the leaves darker and more confident; then, finally, colonised by a tangled growth which blocked the view of the sea. Into one of these clumps Marnie now forced her way. Still wet from the morning's sea fog, upwards of a dozen trunks emerged at strange, secret angles from the shingle to form an organic structure, the whole being less dense than it seemed from the outside, and littered inside with shrivelled leaves, cans empty but uncrushed, bits and pieces of faded blue nylon netting, rich with the smell of human urine. She kept her things inside her tote; after a good rest, took some time to make a hole in the shingle, which, though flattened long before by commercial sex traffic, turned out to be less compressed than she expected. Into this she inserted Phillip's pistol, still wrapped in Phillip's socks, covering it up like an animal, squatting over the hole and scraping towards herself with both hands.

*

At first, she felt relieved to be rid of it. Then, in the middle of the night, regretting the whole idea and thinking she could hear something make its way out of the water and on to the land, she dug it up again, determined to wait until daylight came or face whatever happened. Nothing did, though next morning she found a few shallow scrapes in the shingle around the oak, and wondered if it had only been Andrew, the lost Basuto, disoriented and seeking a human being to connect with, someone who might return him to the happinesses – the small dependable things – his life had once known. In the following days, as she made her way across the grain of the chalk, she often heard abandoned dogs in the maze of lanes behind the sea. The more middle-class hamlets – each with its pond, its cenotaph, its twelfth-century ragstone church boasting original box pews and frost-heaved exterior verticals, its sunny, perfect location at a forgiving bend in the road – were overrun with them. If she could ever pick Andrew out from the pack, she supposed, it would be less a sighting than an act of the imagination. An admission that she was as lost as they were.

Coastal time

—

In the beginning – if there could be said to have been a beginning – no one really understood what had happened.

There was a decade of confusion. Populations declined across the board, as you would expect given the accompanying economic changes. All along the coast, the little places that had made an income from retirees and weekenders – from tourism in general, from a proximity to remnant medieval priories or bijou nature reserves compiled out of two or three acres of hawthorn scrub, a pond and the possible presence of a locally occurring frog – fell in on themselves. By the time things came back into focus, the climate had changed. Geography had changed. Everyone had a different idea about that. Social media was as useless as ever, and though the war with the iGhetti continued, people could never agree on what kind of a war it was, or what its boundaries were.

Coastal time always lags behind. In places like this one – which had previously thought of itself as a convenient weekend refuge two hours south-east of the Square Mile, comprising two pubs, a terrace of flint-faced almshouses and a Queen Anne vicarage, organised around a small but somehow spacious square – it seemed to stretch out and pass even more slowly than before. The cemetery, like an old walled garden, abutted the vicarage; behind both, the original cobbled twittens ran down through a break in the cliffs to where a river drained itself across a wide flat muddy windswept inlet. Not quite a beach but perfect for dog walkers. Towards the end of the 1970s, the almshouses had been knocked together into a Museum of the Sea, featuring objects netted unintentionally by trawlers working the Dogger Bank; thereafter, the relaxed spaces of the original village were quickly infilled by a town's worth of gift shops, delis and minimarts, while retirement suburbs stealthily surrounded both.

During the arrival of the iGhetti, the river had swept down through the local golf course, carrying away garden fences and clumps of pampas grass, leaving behind tangles of blanched and broken branches, plastic bags, used condoms, sewage outfall, broken toys and garden furniture from the dwellings upstream. No one had ever cleaned up, and the suburbs, previously running all the way down to the petrol-coloured water, now ended twenty or thirty yards further inland, having ceded themselves to a mudbank out of which surviving homes emerged empty and stripped clean. Tucked in next to them, where the land climbed cliffs and grassy ramps towards the downlands, a row of half a dozen detached Edwardian houses – each comprising three apartments with large rooms and sea views, still weathertight and comfortable – watched the sea from an ancient alluvial bench.

Early evening. A car arrived by the river, worked its way carefully along the unadopted road that served the houses, and stopped. A figure not unlike a child got out and began dancing. A voice called, 'Get back in here.' A curious light lay across the inlet, glancing off the river, which had fanned out exhaustedly and become so shallow it might have been a coat of varnish applied between the low darkening cliffs. Flakes of what looked like snow flurried across the mud, driving the little figure to run about shouting and splashing, stopping suddenly at intervals to stare back at its own footprints filling with water. Every so often it bent from its hips with its face thrust forward and its arms spread out and back as if it imagined itself in flight. Eventually the adult took hold of it by one arm and dragged it back to the car. A rear door slammed and locked. 'Don't touch anything or I'll shoot you,' the adult warned, and made his way towards the cottages, where the lights were already on and music could be heard. Everything looked as if it were being viewed from the wrong distance, like a scene in a film.

An ash party

—

ALICE MENARD HAD REMOVED ALL but the major load-bearing walls of her ground-floor apartment. It had been less an aesthetic decision, she was always willing to explain, than a bet against gravity. The front door now opened directly from an enclosure of raked pebbles and sea kale – its original Japanese sensibilities blurred off by growths of nobilis and cape daisy – into a space a little too big to be domestic but rather too small to be anything else. This was now full of tired-looking couples with three- and four-year-old children; a party was in progress. 'Oh, look at this old story at the door,' Alice called back to the grown-ups. 'Can anyone think how to sell it?' A few of the women laughed. They had worked for her in media, when media was still an option. 'The legend that is Tennent,' she said, keeping her body between him and the room. He couldn't see anyone he recognised.

Eventually, Tennent knew, she would relent and let him in. Meanwhile she stared him in the eye and announced to the room in general, 'I want you to go to the window and tell me what you see!' The children, unsure they were being addressed, looked surprised then milled about, sturdy and thoughtful, but aimless, as if they had forgotten where the windows were. You could tell they were actual children, not artefacts, from the natural way they wore their copies of the parental styles.

'Snow!' they all called. 'It's snowing!'

'That's right.' Alice applauded. 'It's snowing. And if you're good, we'll make a snowman!'

'Has Hampson been here looking for me?' Tennent said.

'That creep,' she said. 'He was around this afternoon, but he's not here now. Come in and have a drink.'

They went and sat on a sofa: peered out towards what had once been Doggerland. In that direction, the sea had now vanished into a kind of whirling mist lit from within – like a greyscale Turner unearthed in a barn, a lucky post-apocalyptic find.

'It's an ash cloud,' he told her. 'Ash! Any kind of chemistry could be going on in there. Breakdown products of whatever the iGhetti are up to in London. It could be anything. Don't they know?'

'Of course they know,' she said. 'Tennent, I know too.'

'These are their children,' Tennent insisted.

'I expect they'd be happy to have you remind them of that,' she said, perhaps to remind him that he knew nothing about families or children – and, probably, nothing about happiness either.

An hour later, the party showed no signs of abating. The lights went down. The karaoke machine was taking hard use. The adults moved the furniture to one side so they could dance in the middle of the floor; the children ran about between them, chanting and mimicking a popular set of gestures. Tennent, who had felt purposeless and befuddled as soon as he understood the situation, now felt as if he was forgetting why he had come at all. Alice drifted away to dance with a very small girl whose upturned face was illuminated with delight. He was almost glad to see Hampson arrive – a tall, thin man, slipping in without having appeared to open the door, then looking around warily as he leaned against a wall wiping his mouth. Tennent regarded this performance without sympathy, making no attempt to catch his attention. Eventually Hampson came over and tried to speak, his voice nasal and muffled, as if the air in the room were full of water. Before he could get out more than a greeting, Tennent – already beginning to believe they were caught in the same bad patch, enacting some experience neither of them had ever had, let alone shared, each half recognising yet not quite knowing the other – warned him, 'For fuck's sake. Not in here.'

Outside, Hampson stared into the back of the car, wiped his mouth again, then took a few quick, unsteady steps away, as if he didn't want to be caught near Tennent or the item. Tennent got him by the elbow and half led, half pulled him out across the mud until they came to a stop, panting, with water seeping up round their feet.

'Well? Do you want it or not?'

The ash fall was abating. Five or six centimetres of the stuff, uncertain of chemistry and as feathery as the waste from a chicken factory, could now be seen to have covered the mud. The clouds fell back quickly to either side of the sky; light from a waning moon filled the inlet. Behind the two men – who stood regarding one another with a kind of stuck puzzlement – Alice's front door spilled yellow light and children. Hampson walked in a circle, and in a circle again; he said something that Tennent couldn't catch. The children, bundled warmly into puffa jackets, lively scarves and knit stocking caps, began jumping violently about in the ash. They scooped it up and threw it at one another. Their parents built a fire, launched flights of bottle rockets. Alice's sound system boomed out an anthem from their glory days, for the duration of which Alice struck a pose, raising aloft a marine distress flare. Fierce rose-coloured reflections slid and fluttered away from the polished bodywork of the SUVs parked along the service road, but not from the matt grey finish of Tennent's car, which started up suddenly and crept away. The adults sang 'Happy Birthday' to one of their number, and handed round sparklers. Soon, in a curiously touching effort at cooperation, intense yet disconnected, the children would begin building an ashman.

At the Houses of Sunlight

—

WHOEVER HE WAS – AND it was hard to be sure – Hampson claimed to have been inside the City of London and there viewed the iGhetti at close quarters. No one believed him.

He occupied an old rectory at the end of a half-mile metalled drive on the edge of the Downs, next to three or four acres of flat-roofed, red-brick, single-storey structures – the remnants of some late Victorian corporate utopia or model village originally called 'The Houses of Sunlight'. No church could be found for ten miles in any direction. Since an abrupt change of use at the outset of the Second World War, the whole site had been contained by a dense scrub mosaic and some rusty chain-link. Medium-sized satellite dishes, added in the Cold War panics of the early 1980s, loomed over the sheds and lean-tos built to contain Hampson's experimental subjects fifty years later – no longer aiming themselves at the remains of the NATO orbital communications net, but at a selection of extrasolar locations from which he believed the iGhetti might originate. Anxiety lay over it all, expressing itself best in the disconnect between the rectory – plain, four-faced and isolated, yet so obviously domestic in nature – and the model village, with its history of abandonment and re-uptake, its grid of rippled-concrete roadways and internal checkpoints, its dead sparrows in empty rooms. The UK's last coherent administration had earmarked it as a refugee camp; six months later, small-boat traffic on the Channel routes had subsided to a trickle then reversed, like a kind of backed up plumbing of the collective soul. Hampson had lived at the rectory all his life. His own history was opaque until the iGhetti made their transit to Earth. At that point, he had begun to keep notebooks and records.

'For god's sake, Hampson,' said Tennent.

They had come up from the town without speaking. Tennent had addressed the task of driving instead, redlining the engine in a bitterly exact fashion between each blind bend along the chalk lanes. Every change of direction made him feel weightless, relieved and inconsequential. The same motion caused Hampson to grip his seat and blink into the tilted chaos of hedges and gates whitened by the headlights, while in the back of the vehicle, thrown from side to side like a sack of organs, the artefact had lost volition and was having difficulty in responding to requests. Catching sight of it from time to time in the rear-view mirror, Tennent had wondered again if anything real was occurring.

Now he stood staring down the gloomy perspective of what had once been a twenty-metre polytunnel – dirty, baked into opacity by the years of sunlight, but still weatherproof and filled with two rows of ancient hospital beds, each lit by a naked forty-watt bulb. It was hot, and a faint, complex smell hung in the air: not chemical, not organic. If he once allowed himself to recognise it, Tennent felt, he would be lost. He would have to run out of there and not return. Each bed supported an artefact from the sea. The more recognisable of them had the size and slick white unformed appearance of Henry Moore's 1930 *Mother and Child*. Others looked like brown plasticine caught trying to evolve into a human being; seen in the corner of your eye, they were never the same shape twice. From every bed a heavy-duty wiring loom emerged, feeding to a single black cable as thick as Tennent's forearm, which snaked off down the long axis of the polytunnel and out the door. The tunnel, plugged into the universe this way via the nearest satellite dish, felt clogged with whispers, two-way communications traffic you could take in but never make sense of.

'Do you want this thing or not?' Tennent said.

Hampson ignored him; touched the artefact with his hands in two or three places until he found the correct pressure point. When it fell on the floor in a heap, he looked relieved.

'They have to be switched off before you can start modifying them. Let alone connecting them up. Help me get it over there.'

Hampson took the shoulders. Tennent took the feet. Between them, they half carried, half dragged it over to an empty bed, where some deep reflex switched it on again, causing it to curl up with its arms locked firmly around its knees. A struggle ensued. Hampson, Tennent and the artefact rolled this way and that. The artefact squealed and flailed around incoherently each time they got it back on the bed and forced it to straighten out. Every so often it would slump forward, cease responding, or go rigid and tremble. Once it had quietened down, Hampson switched off all the lights but one. He had remained patient and calm throughout, though he was breathing heavily. A quality of the reduced light emphasised the size of his hands. Out of use, they had looked old and clumsy; in use, they were deft, competent, accustomed to whatever minor procedure he was about to perform on the artefact. During a lull in the struggle, it had looked Tennent straight in the eye and said in a clear, precocious voice, 'But I don't want this hand, I want a real one.' The memory of this threw him into a rage.

'I said I'd bring it here,' he told Hampson, 'so here it is. Whatever you're up to, I don't want to be involved.'

'Do what you like,' Hampson advised him absently.

He was peeling back the undeveloped lips of the item and

peering into what passed for a mouth. After a moment or two, he seemed satisfied.

'Come back tomorrow,' he said, 'and I'll tell you if it's any good to me.'

Hampson's notebooks

—

Wednesday, March 4th, 6.40 a.m.: I hate to dream. When the work isn't going well, I dream I'm fat, fat and hard like an armadillo or half a barrel. I dream I'm dead. Sleep becomes tiring. Dreams of loss are nothing new, but they come with new signatures, new styles, raised levels of activity in a place you can't reach, as if your psyche has made new decisions.

Monday, 26th July, 2.30 p.m.: Two scintillating scotoma events this week. I never get migraines, only this, their logo: a clever little neon staircase which starts as a point source, curves around on itself into a broken circle, then slowly and dignificdly, across halt an hour, cxpands until it sccms to havc got bigger than my visual field can contain. At which it might, therefore, be said to have vanished. I'm not sure it has. First, there's a further half hour of minor dyslexia and unclear speech potholed with spoonerisms and aphasia. I believe it takes the aura another twenty-four hours to disperse from the invisible zones. I imagine it expanding steadily, like some low-energy interstellar shock front shining out into the dark. During that time I'm lethargic and warm, suspect I might get a headache but don't. Taste metal, feel a tingling in (of all places) my lips. I used to panic, now I don't. Two decades and it's never changed its nature or its strange, almost magical cycle. Once or twice every six months. Maybe it's even a necessity, some toll I pay for being connected to the other world.

[Undated & defaced]: The other world doesn't make sense. I know that because I've seen into it nightly. In some way, to some extent, I've seen the things that go on there. They make no sense. Are they incompletely rendered? Or simply incomplete? Are they incompletely understood by us, or are they just not understandable in some absolute sense? Theoretical models argue that these other universes are by definition so imperfectly formed as to be untenable. Attempts to go there fail to absurdity, even as thought experiments. We might as well call them 'the astral plane' and be done with it: many have. And yet the iGhetti arrived here (wherever that is) from somewhere and can only be said to be – in some sense – real. So what is happening? Are we watching a film the universe is showing itself?

To book your seat at the cinema you don't need much: I have some receivers in the compound, and some parallel processors in a room upstairs. I slept in that room from the age of four. It was the sort of place you put a child; later it might become a box room. I remember a coloured print of *The Light of the World.* I had the furniture out of there as soon as I was old enough, and burnt it in the yard. One thing I remember is waking in the night to the slow, nauseous tick of the alarm clock, a thick heavy smell of talcum powder – Ashes of Roses – as if my mother had just left. When I was a child, there was always a kind of sticky slowness in the passing of time in that room. Now, unconstrained by the literalism of the old clock, time moves in different ways, and the air smells only of the hot dust recirculated by the system fans.

Tuesday, December 31st: A curious kind of light, in which several colours were represented but only faintly, came and went all day on the other side of the monitors, tingeing the paper I was writing on. Extensive floods down in the valley. Everything disordered or swept away. Worse every year; flood or drought. The Downs: a geomorphology of mysterious wooded lumps in perpetual winter twilight. To an outsider I must resemble a cat, always looking behind the VDU for the object in the image. Fireworks every year at this time, flickering intermittently across the darkness. They seem to pass behind the shoulder of the Downs, backlighting the curve, illuminating faintly the grey walls of my house.

September 9th, 11.47 a.m.: Last night, four out of ten monitors were full of chaos. (A certain amount of random noise in the system pumps the incoming signal by stochastic resonance; although after a point, much as in life, noise is only noise.) Five were blank. Until you looked at it closely, the tenth seemed to be showing an image of the room itself, from the point of view of a cheap webcam mounted high up in one corner. But things weren't entirely right with the wallpaper for it to be this room, and the person sitting there wasn't me. After a moment or two, someone else seemed to enter. The original figure turned its head slowly and began to stand up, perhaps in some kind of clumsy welcoming gesture. Then everything vanished. I ran some comparisons with older data, to see if I had received anything like it before. Nothing. These kinds of images are the least dependable, although sometimes easier to see. Poor reception is only part of the problem. The rest is the unreadability of the information, the difficulty of deriving any meaning from iGhetti transmissions. For instance, how do they make sense of the world? If we don't understand that, how can we make sense of them? For me, the work falls into two parts: to keep the system running – in a sense, to keep reinventing it, or allowing it to reinvent itself – and to understand what we see.

Tuesday, February 3rd: . . . that evening, one of the ordinary receivers was making sounds loud enough to be heard over the wind. Wondered if I should go over to the outbuilding where I keep them, then decided not to. Most of them would need replacing soon anyway. I sat in the kitchen, drinking tea and listening, then went to bed. This morning I could still hear it. You don't want problems at that end of the system. Problems at that end are always time-consuming so I put on my coat and went up to look at it. Very few actual medical procedures seem to be necessary to maintain a receiver once it is up and running. I use a bucket of disinfectant every two days, one or two injections of penicillin. The wiring, the other technical procedures, even the very selection of the original subject, all seem to have a preservative effect. What do I mean by this? Well, not that I am simply picking the durable ones. I mean that being chosen confers a certain quality of metaphysical endurance the subject may not have possessed in their ordinary life. Of course an organic toughness is helpful: and they often surprise me with that. Some don't last out the first two or three days – those I always recognise, and dispose of quickly. But others seem so frail and last so long. I checked the wiring, and the optical pipe which carries the signal across to the system. All good.

[Date illegible, except perhaps '12th']: There may be some question that the iGhetti is a single entity made up of a huge number of components with variable functions. Immediately after the invasion, hundreds of thousands of these were discarded everywhere. The seas are still full of them, like a stew. Our perspectives on this monster have been shadowy, parallactic, indeterminate. All the crimes – and there have been so many – have taken place in the face of – under the auspices

of – the confusion caused by the iGhetti: but none of it is ever treated as their crime. It is, at its most explicable, human activity caught up and whirled about by the turbulence of *activity at another level*; the only direct link between the iGhetti and us is the damage they have caused to First World infrastructures. We know nothing about their actual intentions, or about any traceable line of causality between our actions and theirs. *They may not even know we are here.* Until this became clear, we pretended our scientific episteme was still serviceable, or that a serviceable episteme might be arrived at by methods we'd used previously. It was an intellectual ghost dance. After that, the apocalypse seemed to withhold itself, quickly becoming just another historical continuity. That is to say, we got used to it. No one had expected the utter banality of that.

Midnight, Friday, September 6th: When you talk about your parents, you aren't really talking about people. You're talking about some force or organising principle in your life. Everything has contributed to it, including acts of unrelated human beings, and even of your own, which had nothing to do with them. You call that whole complex 'your parents', because it originated with them. Any fresh input gets mixed up with them, fusing into a substrate from which you emerge different but the same. My parents seemed paralysed. They never bought their own house. They never moved from this one, although they always had plans; so many plans, even at the end. Afterwards I bought the house. I bought the outbuildings. But those two still irritate me, scratching about in their failed life as if they had no right to anything. When I look round this place, I remember the clutter of it before I took possession.

[No date, some charring]: It's sometimes quite affecting when a receiver tries to speak to you. By then, they can't communicate, of course. They make their whistlings and flutings, an occasional gargling or gagging noise. What do they see, if they see anything? The same future as my instruments? Or something else altogether? Their experience, after all, is as the detector, not the data it receives. There's a central distinction here. Their subjectivity, if they retain one, consists in being whatever the iGhetti built them to be – and we don't even know what that is.

[No date, extensively charred]: Down in the town, behaviour comes in discrete knots. Long before the iGhetti arrived, everyone was playing out a separate fantasy. Unable to pretend to sleep and suddenly needing something familiar, I go and sit with the system. There isn't much help there. Less and less is familiar any more, I realise. I no longer belong to myself, let alone anyone else. A dangerous condition to be in. In the morning, I sit on the sofa and the sun shines across my eyes, making it impossible to concentrate. Time draws out. This isn't the first time I've felt alienated in this house. I'm still grinding my teeth.

Sunday, August 12th: This! From a letter of Pierre Curie to Georges Gouy, April 14th, 1906 – 'In my opinion, there is here a whole domain of completely new facts and physical states of space about which we have had no conception.'

Tuesday, September 24th: As soon as I could after I bought the house, I had the kitchen demolished. It was an ancient extension in a different-coloured brick – more like a scullery – with its huge, ancient sink. Carbolic soap, green chenille tablecloth, long drawn-out nauseas of food and smells and boredom. From it, you could only enter the old garden, walled, narrow as an alley, with a bluish brick path and barley sugar brick edgings to the vegetable bed. This brick had a hard finish, a metallic, clinkered look. Rusted buckets upturned over rhubarb. The smell of that, and the smell of the roses and sunshine and dust. There aren't many anagrams of the word insect.

[No date, heavy charring]: I suppose I just want to give them a voice.

On the beach in the Square Mile

—

TENNENT DROVE BACK DOWN THROUGH the folded landforms in the moonlight. Every third corner they gave him a glimpse of the sea – predictably silver – or a field with sheep. Flakes of ash hovered at a distance in the headlights, then rushed at him playfully and raced away behind. By the time he reached Alice's home, the festivities were drawing out, slowing down: the fireworks were over. The children, sensing that the party was over for them too, ran about in the garden, desperate to preserve those last intense moments – changing direction suddenly, pushing one another over, shouting and writing preliterate phrases on the dark with bits of smouldering wood. Inside, the lights were turned up full, revealing the remains of an ugly cake, half eaten on plates or trodden into the floor. He found

Alice standing thoughtfully by the window, as if she hadn't moved.

'Christ,' she said, 'you look awful. I thought you'd gone.'

'I had,' Tennent said. 'I had gone. Now I'm back and I want a drink.'

Alice was thinner than usual, but her face retained a solid look, shrewd and a little thick-lipped, as if it belonged to someone larger, a few years older and already bored with him. Children burst into the room behind them, laughing and raising their arms to the adults to have their smeary coats and boots taken off. She watched them for a moment, while Tennent found a bottle of Scotch and poured some of it into a used glass.

'I hate parties,' he said.

'You don't change.'

'On the contrary,' Tennent advised her. 'I never stay still.'

'Do you want to come to bed with me?'

He swallowed his drink.

'Can we eat something first?'

There wasn't much you could say about this relationship, Tennent believed, except that its sole purpose seemed to be to describe itself, which in practice meant a rolling re-inscription of the interludes long or short between their encounters, also the reasons for them. They ate what he had rescued from the party refuse, drank the whisky, lay watching a fresh squall of ash blow in across the estuary. Once or twice, they wrapped their arms around one another in an experimental way. These kinds of discussions had, in the past, lasted all night. He wanted to be told who the people at the party were; she wanted to know if he was off the beach and looking to be taken in. Before he could answer no to that, she pushed him away and got off the bed and went to the window.

'How's Marnie?' she said suddenly.

'Marnie's fine.'

Ash-light filled the room. It was a kind of light, he thought, that negated them both. It made everything remote from everything else.

'You haven't been there for weeks.'

'I was there only two days ago,' he said. 'She insisted on feeding me as if I was fourteen. She couldn't remember what a robin was called.'

'I hate you sometimes.'

'Perhaps it was three days. I could be wrong.'

She turned away from the window but remained in front of it, the light spraying round her on its way to him. 'I'm sailing,' she said. 'Tomorrow.'

'Jesus, Alice.'

'I've had enough of it all. If you wanted to act like a human being for once, you could give me a lift to the port.'

Later, she fell asleep. Tennent moved away from her in the bed and lay there remembering a wedding reception many years before, in the garden of a famous Tudor house somewhere along the Thames not far from Richmond. Drunk and bemused, ready to call it a night and go home, tired of the heat, the karaoke, the effect of champagne and the smell of beer, he'd gone out into the grounds. There in the space between the house and the river, he found a dark strip of trampled turf littered with discarded paper plates, plastic forks and used condoms, and in the middle of it, Alice.

Oblivious to everything but her own happiness, she was dancing. Her shoes were off. Laughing and half singing to herself, she dipped and bent and trailed her arms, taking little running steps to some internal music while the lights of Teddington glittered from the opposite shore. On the one hand, it was performative behaviour, he could see; on the other, an undeniable expression of joy. She was twenty-eight years old at that time, working for a Camden media agency. Her husband of an hour or two had recently been paid a million pounds for a single month's work. Tennent felt as if the night had offered him something after all, but it hadn't been intended for him: a private moment but also in some way one beyond his psychological means, something blessed and expensive that he had stumbled into. Later, of course, he realised she had taken E, and was working off the excess energy. When Tennent applauded quietly, she smiled to herself as if she had heard just another of the things down inside her own head.

In those days, many moments had been like that, tainted by leisure chemicals, aspiration, the downwash of celebrity culture, the narcissistic sense of self which had trickled out from university postmodernism in the generation before. To everyone in the marquee, life had been like a huge silent beautiful blossom opening to the economic light, with its roots deep in a mysterious, self-fulfilling growth medium and its leaves outstretched to welcome each new opportunity, untroubled and hothoused until the arrival of the iGhetti from whatever plane of existence they had previously occupied.

After that, no one had known how to act. One minute they heard the sirens, the next they were assured that nothing was happening. One day they were panicking and leaving the city in numbers, the next they were returning but rumour had convinced them to throw their tablet computers in the river. The thing they feared most was contagion. They locked their doors. They severed their broadband connections and tanked their cellars. They avoided a growing list of foods. They clustered round a smartphone every summer evening after dark, eavesdropping on the laconic WhatsApp conversations of the local militias as they scoured the railway banks and canalsides for telltale astral jelly. Were the iGhetti here or not? Otherwise, they were trying to live a normal life. It was a difficult time for everyone.

Tennent, by then in his early twenties and up to town

for good from an unfinished PPE degree at Oxford, lived in a rented room, ate with the family and phoned his mother once a week or so before he went to bed. During the day, he hung around in coffee shops and cafes, but allowed her to believe he worked in a fourteenth-floor office in the stub of the Undershaft, doing publicity for a fuel corporate. 'It's nice,' he told her. 'Quite heads-down but worth it to have the security.' He didn't know why he lied to her about that, or failed to admit that his real life took place at weekends, in a gentrified warren on the edge of the Square Mile, where Alice, her marriage to the millionaire now carefully folded away in case she needed it later, lived with a man called Jack. Jack had made a success out of reinsurance no one else would touch, diverting some of his considerable gains into a silk weaver's house from the early 1700s. That house had been his project of the heart, Jack claimed, but now it was finished, he was often away. 'Jack has affairs of his own,' Alice would say, with a wry look, and leave it hanging.

The Square Mile, like West London, still believed itself to be intact, functioning – the heart of what had been called, before money failed, an 'economy'. Its pull was still strong for people like Alice and Jack. Brokers from Suffolk continued to commute each morning and, puzzled by the disorder, tried to complete handshake deals at the Coq d'Argent. Finding it hard to place themselves – feeling that the City was in front of them yet not subject to being seen, like some location beyond the reach of satnav – and, still constrained by the concepts both of work and the week, went home to their families at close of play, making the short but by now confusing train journey to Wickham Market.

Everyone knew someone who, unable to bear any longer the loss of their routine, had found their way back into the invasion site, to re-emerge weeks or even months later after wandering puzzledly about the empty towers, lost souls eyeing other lost souls in the deserted corridors and partner washrooms. With a decent pair of binoculars, you could see them from Jack and Alice's garden, staring out of the Lloyds lifts – which still travelled in their stately way up and down the outside of the structure – in despair. In a way, the Lloyds building, designed to question the relationship between the inside and the outside, remained the great metaphor of the disaster. It was the zone's dead centre in that sense, even though it lay towards the western edge.

Tennent was never tempted to include himself in this assessment. Money hadn't drawn him there, he could be sure of that: he didn't have any, and the Square Mile wasn't, as far as he could see, a way for him to get some. Nor had it been his memories of Alice, witchily dancing off the chemicals on the lawn beside the Thames – because he knew he would never be sure what he was to her, other than a release from some innate dissatisfaction, a promise of admiration, a twist of excitement for the weekend. What brought him there was his own drug of choice: the iGhetti themselves, or, more properly, the concept or enigma they represented, as flimsy and enduring as any conspiracy theory. He was sure he would be shown something. Meanwhile, he wandered from room to room of Jack's post-Huguenot fantasy, hypnotised by the strange slow light falling on the original panelling and contrasting twenty-first-century palette of the furnishings. The clean new art filled him with the kind of tranquil delight that only money can buy. In and out of the bedrooms he went, up and down the staircase restored to creak exactly as it had before; past the Sin Wai Kin face-wipe monoprints to pause in awe before the real Cy Twombly.

Alice seemed less content. Her relentless bad tempers set the tone; eventually they all three grew dissatisfied with the arrangement. Jack – who at fifty-eight years old generously viewed both of them as children – came home even less often. Alice shouted at him on the phone. The odd Saturday night he did return, they shouted at one another from different rooms. Tennent, emotionally underprepared for tensions like these, took a dining chair into the garden and spent his evenings with a pair of Leica Geovid Pros, the custom lens coatings of which had, Jack boasted, cost more than his first car. Through them, something could usually be seen moving out there, above the roofline, between the taller buildings. Light artillery airbursts obscured it, but you could tell it was alive. Heavier bursts shook the earth, yet nothing seemed to happen. No buildings fell. It was as if all that happened somewhere else. In cold weather he wore an extra fleece, slightly large on him and smelling of Jack, who followed him out one night and, after fifteen minutes of passing the binoculars back and forth in companionable silence, asked, 'But don't you ever wonder what they want?'

Tennent said he didn't.

'This is only the beginning. They've been here less than a decade.' Jack stared at the City towers for a moment longer, then added, 'If "here" means anything at all. What do they want, Phillip? Everyone wants something. What do they want?'

Suddenly Alice came up behind them. 'I've had enough of it,' she was shouting. 'I've had enough of this.' She put her arms around Tennent and began frantically kissing the back of his neck. He struggled out of her grasp and stood up. By the time they had disengaged, Jack was already back inside, shaking his head and laughing. His interest in them was waning. He had got whatever it was he wanted. You could see that. As far as Jack was concerned, they were no longer players, even minor ones; they were naives – mice, or neuters – in his internal account of life.

'Let's leave,' Alice said.

'What would we do?'

Alice shrugged. 'Go somewhere,' she said.

'But where?'

After a night spent thinking about it, Tennent remembered his aunt Marnie and her house near the sea, and described it to Alice in favourable terms. They left the Square Mile to its own devices and began their long run south, their only luggage a sports bag that someone in Tennent's family had brought back from Sri Lanka in the mid-00s, its thick leather hide dyed a strange orange colour and still stinking inside of whatever process had been used to tan it.

In those days, everyone had a story to tell, but no one could be sure what it was. Tennent's story – the one he told about himself – was that he didn't want certainty. He wasn't sure why. Everything about the iGhetti still enthralled him, but at that time he wanted to live the invasion as it presented itself to him, not as owned by Jack or Alice or anyone else.

Later, when Marnie rehearsed this narrative, she tended to leave Alice out of it.

Sail away

—

TENNENT WOKE UP REMEMBERING THESE things. In turn he woke Alice, who yawned and looked at him as if she didn't know who he was. 'I suppose you want coffee,' she said. He could hardly escape the similarities between their situation then and now. By six they were on their way to the ferry terminal. Mist hung at the corners of the lanes, obscured the passing places, cleared without warning to reveal ill-matched elements of landscape – sheds, trees, raw sodden earth beside a gate. Alice hardly spoke. Tennent, interpreting this as bad temper, drove faster. He was confused by the flat quality of his own memories. Like old comedy films, they seemed to lack meaningful social markers. You wondered why anyone in them was doing the things they did – you wondered what you were supposed to infer. He listened instead to the engine noise, for reliable clues to the state of his car.

'For god's sake,' Alice said, when he tried to explain, and even that sounded as if she was talking to herself.

Down at the terminal, lines of refugees waited to sail. Families with wheeled luggage, unaccompanied children with backpacks. Tennent stopped to watch them for a moment. Most of them would have driven down from the city overnight, staring hard out of the windscreens to avoid the faint, iridescent blur in the air at a T-junction or the bottom of a hill that signalled a bad patch. They had got rid of decent houses in Hackney or Hammersmith for whatever they would fetch, and the SUVs they had sold as soon as they arrived were drawn up in rows outside the dock, under the boarding gate signs. They looked tired but relieved, outfitted in smart casual as if for a day at the office. Their anxieties were beginning to dissolve in the salt sunshine. At the same time, they gave off an air of not being entirely involved in what they were doing or the decision-making that had led to it. Their needs had changed, and along with them, the associated fears. Their attention was spread too thin; in lag. If you got into a bad patch, things could be pushed out of shape very quickly, then even more quickly spring back into place again. It was hard to say which was the more unnerving.

Travel guides, understanding this, moved among them,

organising manageable groups, calling out names, taking money, offering paper tickets of a kind the world had not seen for a while. It was sometimes possible to catch sight of the Gauf brothers passing between the queues or examining the parked vehicles. All of this bustle and purpose, Tennent thought, belonged to them, though it seemed to him to lead only to one place: the towering hull of the boat, the end of a narrow, steeply angled gangplank without safety rails. After that, a series of the vaguest possibilities: the cramped cabin; the seasickness; a mist and the passage into nowhere.

'I hate ships,' he said. 'Are you sure you want to do this?'

Alice looked at him with contempt, then, after some effort, smiled.

'Come with me,' she suggested. And then when he didn't answer: 'I mean it. Come with me.'

'There's nothing out there.'

'There must be something,' she argued. 'There's nothing wrong with the rest of the world, you can be sure of that. It's only this shithole. Come with me.' She glanced back inland, to where the chalk rolled away north and light glinted off aircraft high up. 'We didn't ask for this. It wasn't meant to be like this.'

Tennent didn't know how to reply.

Eventually she shook her head. 'What I'm trying to say is that we all feel cheated now,' she said. 'I don't know why you need to make such a production out of it.' When he didn't answer, she said, 'Do you think if I waited a day or two, Marnie would come? She shouldn't be here on her own.'

Tennent shrugged. 'Who knows what Marnie will do?'

The queue seemed endless, but they didn't speak again. He waved to her as she dragged her luggage up the gangplank high above the foul mud, and she waved back energetically. He saw she was relieved to go, whatever might happen.

'Bye!' he called. 'Bye!'

Ghost responsibilities

—

MARNIE THOUGHT SHE HEARD THE lost dog barking.

For thirty-six hours, steep cliffs descending directly into the water had forced her away from the shoreline, where there was no path even when the tide was low. Afternoon, and the sun could be seen pale and chalky above the remains of the morning's fog as she trudged up between the silent beech trees and wandered about calling, 'Andrew! Andrew!' Every time she called, the dog stopped barking to listen, only to start again from another quarter of the wood.

Desire paths ran everywhere up there. They were deeply ingrained and damp, and they wound between mysteriously chosen landmarks – trampled hollows with a small pool and a pile of branches, little caches of broken household objects – as if made by children. Her coat was muddy; her hands all mud from falling forward on the slope. Her walking shoes were caked with it. 'Andrew!' she called. By then she had no idea which way she was facing. Fallen trees were everywhere. They lay across one another, still alive, a hundred feet in length, still flourishing from their minimal contact with the earth in the aftermath of some unimaginably violent disturbance. Several of these beached-looking leviathans could be found in a single glade, many with younger trees growing from the earth caked in their ripped-up root boles, so that at moments in the weak grey light it looked as if a different species was springing out of the polished grey carcass of the original.

Birch from beech, Marnie thought, holly from ash. A sense of terror overcame her. The bared roots of the saplings seemed to resemble the tubes – part hydraulic, part intestinal, part muscular – that no one can ignore in the drawings of H. R. Giger. Marnie hurried on past this display of the visceral sublime, whispering, 'We just need to get out of the woods,' as though she had already taken charge of the dog. She had adopted its owner's baggage and all that stemmed from it – responsibilities that, if not exactly foisted upon her, had been unfairly passed on as the ghost of a single encounter.

The exhausted light faded from hour to hour. It was beginning to fail as she found her way down to the sea again, along wide shallow valleys and into one of the well-known seasonal waterside art towns of Kent. Rain blew into her face. She was exhausted. There were aches in her shoulders and upper back. There was no dog. There is no mud to struggle through like chalk mud.

The gallery

—

THE iGHETTI HAD SOLVED – so they claimed – many of the issues we associate with the mathematics of Grothendiecke and Mochizuki.

By way of those solutions, they gained access not just to the astral plane, but to the even more complex and distant spaces beyond. Their relations with such spaces were controlled through architecture, either their own or that of the human builds that most attracted them. As a result, on a coast so fully dedicated to the arts – and thus to fresh new museums, performance halls and galleries – it had always been hard to tell these alien structures from their nearest human equivalent. The iGhetti were rarely, if ever, found in them, so what they were used for was, like everything else, a matter of speculation.

It was as if, initially at least, they had been determined to demonstrate – not simply to us but to themselves – that they had something of us in them. From Hastings round to Thanet and the North Foreland, new builds set out to combine the wafery values of the wasp nest with the disconnected perspectives of a postmodern waste disposal facility in Gloucestershire. They were often a silvery colour, or featured sheaves and fans of wavelength-sensitive glass. They redistributed light along mysterious channels. Some were sited on distinctive and highly visible points such as cliffs and headlands, inshore islands or chalk ridges in the near hinterlands; others hidden in landscape folds or back streets. From whatever direction you approached, they most often resembled a cluster of buildings rather than a single one, viewed from an 'inexplicable' – that is, not anthropocentric – angle. You came upon them slowly, across a morning's walk, appearing and disappearing from sight like the lighthouses of a new kitsch, or, in town, discovered them inserted into sudden, windy, peculiarly graceful spaces between amusement arcades and Korean restaurants.

The building that now rose before Marnie looked less like a gallery than a funeral home she had once glimpsed from a dull beach strewn with blackened seaweed at Alicante, during that restless, aggravated season before the iGhetti broke through – when people felt uncomfortable inside their own skin but didn't yet know why. That was the final day of what would turn out to be her – and perhaps everyone else's – final fortnight in Spain. 'I liked it,' she would write to Phillip when she finally got home through the chaos. 'No. I was *entranced* by it.' She had been entranced by the tanatorio's inappropriate cylindrical build and tall curved windows, decorated on the outside with a panoramic mural in the style of a woodcut and featuring the dead silhouetted by the invisible sun of the afterlife.

'Their shadows were attenuated, vast. I was entranced by those melodramatic perspectives. But when I went in, I found that the foyer had been given over to a month-long retrospective of a newly rehabilitated analytic cubist. Can you imagine! A misogynist in a funeral parlour!'

She preferred, she wrote, the painter's early work: the cracked and sea-worn wooden panel of *Fernande with Mantilla*, like an icon retrieved from a wreck; his partial human beings, as in the unfinished *Woman Watching Her Sleeping Male Companion*, in which the incongruously bright colours of the male torso made it seem less real – less present – than the faint monochrome of the pencilled figure emerging from the background; and a small canvas, entitled *Sleeping Nude* but clearly representing a bowl of fruit with a pink lobster claw protruding, the fruit done in the glossy colours of *pintura domestica*.

Up close it had a kind of cheerful brutality. 'His gaze,'

she concluded, 'is less a gaze than a ruthless disregard. But it leaks into the real – and then everything you know has folded itself according to some aesthetic you barely understand, and in the process lost its function.' The temporariness of that, she thought, was aggravating in itself. 'Within minutes you've given yourself permission to shrug, walk away and never engage again.'

At that time she had no sense that Phillip would receive her email. Europe was busily collapsing in the face of change. There was a vigorous ambiguity to everything. For Marnie – not entirely able, even then, to separate the demented from the actual – such hybrid architectures of feeling had converged even as they seemed to separate, linked by the same physics of the absurd.

Back in the Kentish present, she stood looking up at the gallery's complex curtain wall. The wind groaned around the base of it. Inside she went, quickly wiping the rain off her face and trying not to think, and sat down awkwardly but gratefully in the atrium to rest her arthritic hip. When the sun was low, long shadows split all the rooms. Evening came on but not the lights. Patches of shattered glass and framing materials lay in corners. Empty areas of floor remained cordoned off as if they still contained something. It's hard to relax when every space opens on to another. She slept in a corner of the inevitable gift shop, under a pile of Mondrian-themed cycling jerseys for warmth, and dreamed she was out between the houses on the seafront, struggling in a strong hot wind with a medium-sized dog. She woke kicking the nearest wall hard enough to bloody her toes. The animal was still there, a kind of beige colour, with sick, winsome eyes. It was a prolonged engagement, but by dawn she was properly awake again, if a little uneasy about the way the early light fell into one room from another or from a corridor you couldn't see. Some things can only be intuited. The blood had vanished, but the wall was still somehow slick with all the qualities of three in the morning. Her toes were unmarked, so perhaps that had been part of the dream too.

She wandered about all day, impatiently turning over the remains of the art. Birds had got in and were whirring calmly about high up in the atrium. Outside, as the weather improved, people could be seen wandering back and forth through the layers of light and distance. It was often the same family group, walking up and down, up and down the beach. Every so often, one of the children would crouch to examine a shell. She wondered what they had done for their holidays before the disaster, if 'the disaster' was what you were expected to call it. No one came in. In the afternoon, after finally reassuring herself that the gallery had been abandoned for months, she returned to the gift shop and began to collect the materials she would need. She felt swollen and hurt in some place she couldn't locate. She wouldn't forget the look in the animal's eyes. It had been, she thought, as complicit as she was. Other than that, she felt that the art museum would make an acceptable, even an interesting, new home.

The mystic vigil

—

TENNENT DECIDED HE WOULDN'T SELL the item to Hampson after all.

When he returned to the rectory on the Downs, he found the two of them in one of the upstairs rooms. Thick curtains were closed, so that the illumination came mainly from the obsolete CRT monitors set up on every flat surface, ten or a dozen of them linked through a rat's nest of cable. It was an ugly kind of light, flattening and at the same time suggestive. The item lay on its back on the floor as if it had been arranged that way by someone attentive and full of care, one arm placed across its chest, its new hand very detailed and lit as if separately. The air was warm, and Hampson's head seemed to be too big. It was distorted in some way. At first you put that down to the light, then you thought it might be the angle of the head to the high, stooped shoulders. Then you thought it might be reminding you of a painting. Hampson was crouched on the floor beside the artefact. He folded his knees awkwardly underneath him. Groaned. He seemed to be unhinging his lower jaw.

Tennent stood in the doorway, looking anywhere but at this tableau. His gaze stuck on another painting, Holman Hunt's *The Light of the World*. He could see it on one of the monitors, in a poor-contrast greyscale through which thick swirls of interference came and went. At the same time he could see it framed on the wall above the monitor, a print in a cheap frame, full of warm gold hues: a figure, perhaps Jesus, raises aloft a lantern with one hand and, with the other, taps furtively on a Gothic door while it glances over its shoulder at something in the nearby weeds.

'Hampson, what are you doing?' he made himself say.

A laugh. A gesture which seemed to take in everything near – the room, its contents, the item and its fresh new hand.

'Imagine,' Hampson said, 'not being able to know what you're experiencing. By that, I don't mean not being able to understand, but *not being able to know*. Can you imagine that?'

'Yes,' Tennent said, though he couldn't. 'But what are you doing?'

'I'm going through a bit of a bad patch.'

Hampson put his hands under the shoulders of the artefact and pulled it towards him. He seemed to be trying to swallow its head. The artefact had stopped struggling and now stared up passively into his face, its attention caught perhaps by the huge nostrils, the cavernous underside of his lip, the arch of the palate. Hampson's eyes were also passive, sensuous and tired-looking. It was as if the process had calmed them both. Tennent shouted something – he wasn't sure what. He stepped into the room and kicked out. Hampson stared at him puzzledly and then they rolled about angrily, grunting with effort, in the thick carpet of dust under the gaze of *The Light of the World*. At times a shadow surrounded them, in a shade of cobalt blue almost black. Out of that, small white feathers seemed to be spilling, as if someone had burst a pillowcase. Confused by this illumination as much as by the effort of performing violence, they blundered into the tables of monitors, which rocked or fell over. There were brief lulls in the struggle, during the last of which Tennent held Hampson down by the shoulders and stared into his face.

'What are you *doing*?' he said.

'Tennent, nothing's changed inside the Square Mile. It's only from our side of things that it's a war. They don't see it like that. When I was inside, it might have been six o'clock on a summer morning!'

'You were never inside.'

'I could hear the artillery and the bombers outside the zone, but nothing penetrated. Only the "blue effects" told me when one of them was near.' He groaned. 'I'm still in there,' he said.

Tennent laughed. 'You were never inside,' he said.

'I'm telling the truth!' Hampson shouted. 'I'm trying to tell you the truth!' He tore himself from Tennent's grip and ran from the room, down the stairs and out into the primordial secondary growth of the old garden.

Tennent, who felt that he might soon lose his own grasp on events, drew back the curtains so hard they were torn off the rail. Nothing could be seen out there. Inside, the walls of the room were revealed to be papered in a faded pattern of cabbage roses. One or two of the CRTs still worked, but he couldn't make any sense of what they showed. The air smelled of hot plastic recirculated by the system's cooling fans, as if the drive towers had briefly cooked. Behind that could be detected the thick smell of talcum powder, Ashes of Roses, signature fragrance of a vanished old aunt who had last crossed the landing from the bathroom to look for a clean towel at eight o'clock in the evening two generations ago.

Perhaps the most significant item in the room was a loose-leaf journal in a soft black faux-leather cover – squared paper, handwritten in coloured inks, each entry carefully timed and dated – which lay half-open, charred here and there by some inexplicable desktop conflagration – among the tangled wires. Tennent blew the dust off it, read: *a space as full of generated sounds as it was echoes, and no way of telling which was which; a psychological condition more than an environment, offering up objects which seemed to represent it but never did.*

'For fuck's sake,' he said.

If he listened, he could hear Hampson somewhere off in the distance, where he seemed to be setting fire to things at random. His voice hung in the twilight, faint yet raucous.

Tennent threw the notebook down, changed his mind, ploughed his hands in circles through the dust until he found it again. *Believe all you like,* he read, *that at some level unavailable to you an organising principle exists. You will never have any evidence of that.* He rolled it up and jammed it in the pocket of his coat, then he went down the stairs, out of the rectory and into the Houses of Sunlight. The artefact followed, touching him to attract his attention, looking at the things he looked at, pointing back at the upstairs windows as if to draw his attention to a disarray he might not otherwise have noticed. It shyly displayed its new hand, now almost indistinguishable from the original. It seemed quieter than he remembered. He thought its facial features might be a little more distinct.

'Leave me alone,' he said. 'And keep up.'

Several of the original Houses of Sunlight were now on fire. Flames issued from their doors and windows with the static, stylised, distinct quality of flames cut from red and yellow paper. Many of the lean-tos and most of the polytunnels were already down to ash. Confused groans and urgent fluting sounds issued from the remainder; through that chorus, Hampson's voice could be heard, not much different but with an unmistakably entitled edge. Small explosions came and went. Tennent jogged about the site, keeping to the roads and calling Hampson's name to no result. The fires seemed to reflect off the higher slopes of the Downs and the violet- and green-tinged clouds above; you would say that though light had been added to the air, seeing became more, not less, difficult.

The artefact, meanwhile, its cheeks rosy in the firelight, ran to and fro like a long dog, circling away from him then back, but always, it seemed, drawing him towards the edge of the site opposite the rectory. So far, the communications dishes were untouched. With perspective, Tennent thought, you might see how they lined up, in a half-mile row at the end of which the tallest one separated itself from the rest like the dot of an exclamation mark. Here the artefact stopped without warning and stared up, rigid with excitement, as if it had only now noticed the sky and the clean arch of brand new stars revealed with the arrival of the iGhetti. Everyone had loved that to begin with. Now they weren't so certain.

'Oh,' it said.

Tennent attempted to move both of them on and a brief, silent struggle ensued. The item braced itself, bit him almost contemplatively and pulled away, all without removing its attention from the sky. Throughout, its eyes remained firmly closed.

'For god's sake,' said Tennent.

'I don't want to see it, I just want to be it.'

He left it there and wandered about thinking what to do. The dish was thirty or forty feet tall, with support girders jointed and widely set, so that it seemed to crouch above a low windowless, flat-roofed brick building, the door of which hung open on a single large space. Inside he found a tiled and fully washable floor, walls lined with obsolete telemetry equipment, speaker systems in stacked metal boxes with sloping wire fronts. Two or three swivel chairs on casters gave access to gauge boards like eighty-year-old white goods. As soon as he entered, the air filled with a thick musical tone more like a smell or taste than a sound. If he listened hard, he heard something counterpointing that – something that mimicked the hysterical babble of a distant auctioneer, high up in one corner where no speaker was visible. In the centre of the room, someone had installed a thick-walled ceramic feature, rather taller and wider than a bathtub but having similar proportions. The floor tiles were up and two crude channels had been hacked into the poured concrete beneath, one as a conduit for various colours of rubberised cable, the other to carry away waste. Into this receptacle, long before the iGhetti came down, had been packed two naked creatures about the size of adult human beings.

Their faces were human enough. Their heads were thrown back, their mouths gaped. They were aware that they were still alive. Ribcages and abdominal cavities had been opened up as if for massive surgery, the organs collapsed and hollowed out, their surfaces lacquered by the weird light. Though they remained connected, the entrails had been removed and wound like a complex antenna between a series of bobbin-shaped objects placed around the room.

Now that it was too late, Tennent remembered how he had lived on the beach. He began to wonder what had happened to his life since the morning he waded out of that rich surf of objects, soaked to the skin, battered this way and that by sunlit waves he hardly noticed, shaking the spray out of his hair, shouting in delight and with the artefact displayed triumphantly at arm's length above his head. Everyone on the sands had shouted along with him. It was a find, after all. All beachcombers are excited by a find. But they had also recognised – and, down deep, Tennent had recognised too – that he would now be changed. He would no longer be himself, if he had ever been. It's what happens when you get too close to the sea. He remembered the pleasure of it despite that.

But now, he thought, was the time to make decisions about himself. And so he went round the room disconnecting every power cable he could find. At the gauge boards, he turned to Off all the comically obsolete switches in the On position; those in the Off position he turned to On. Anything between, he left. Outside, the communications dish creaked and squealed as it tracked and realigned itself to some random tranche of the sky. In response, the auctioneer in the corner gabbled faster, keen perhaps to make a point before everything went to hell and the window of opportunity closed. The voice still sounded faint and removed. The loose door banged in a light wind.

'Fuck it all,' Tennent said, addressing no one but himself, and was immediately surprised to fetch a response: a clear, echoing tenor voice from the bathtub feature, which enquired, 'Is this the *boy*, Mabel? I can't quite make him out.' It was two or three degrees cooler in there than in the room itself, but nothing had changed. Perhaps nothing ever would. Though he thought its occupants might have managed to move closer to one another, theirs was still an arrangement of static despair and disbelief – a moment of paralysed self-disgust frozen in time yet still somehow moving forward. 'I preferred the girl. The boy was all "new music" and stupid shoes.'

Tennent leaned in.

'Who are you?' he asked.

No answer.

The door banged open and shut again, and from behind him, Hampson said, 'Someone has to try and communicate with them. I already had the technology.' He laughed. 'Although this was an early effort.'

'Are these your parents?'

Instead of replying, Hampson produced a wan smile. 'Just look at me!' he said, making hand movements so dissociated he seemed to be pointing to someone else altogether. His clothes were charred, the left side of his face a single blister. He stank of smoke, and appeared ill but unexhausted; amiable but deserted by his sense of balance. As soon as he had Tennent's attention, he clutched the doorframe with one hand and swivelled carefully around until he could look out and upward without falling over.

'They're coming,' he warned. 'If you care about yourself, you'll leave.'

'Hampson, these are your parents.'

'How do you know that? You can't know that.'

He didn't know anything, Tennent had to admit: he would be the first to agree he had no idea what was going on. Hampson considered this act of surrender for some moments. 'The world's over,' he decided. 'But that doesn't matter. Because another one will be along soon enough.'

'What have you been doing here?'

'I'm not paying you for the item. This fuck-up is very much your fault.'

With that, Hampson laughed again; let go of the doorframe; staggered, caught himself, and lurched away towards a low-lying bank of smoke, into which he vanished only to reappear three or four minutes later moving at a decent clip southwards: a swaying, off-centre figure of sticks on a narrow chalk path in the back of a landscape painted at night. Tennent stared after him. Then he shook his head, collected the artefact from its mystic vigil beneath the big dish and drove back along the coast. Behind him, the sky bloomed silently in a way he would thereafter find difficult to explain to himself: except to say that while the creature that rose into the air was as tall as a cathedral and – there was no other way to put this – had all the powdery, chemical look of a white phosphorous explosion, it manifested in extreme slow motion and was full of busy lights. It hovered momentarily in the air above the Houses of Sunlight before pouring itself away after Hampson, south across the Downs.

Tennent felt that he had moved on; that he had learned something even if he would never be sure what it was. Already he could feel the approach of the beaches he knew, and through the open side window, smell the onshore wind, the vegetation on dry shingle above the tidal zone. It made him think of Alice Menard again, and how they had come down from London together, often travelling by night and on water, learning the beachcombing methods of the little communities through which they passed. That had been an education. An education and, in some sense, an idyll. An idyll until they reached Kent and began to live on the beach together. Phillip liked Alice; Alice liked Marnie; Marnie, for reasons Tennent never understood, loathed Alice.

The sign

—

ON ALL THOSE RELIABLE MAPS of the pre-disaster period, the town assembles itself as a rough triangle, the base of which is a strip of the old coast road running along the seafront for half a mile between a roundabout in the south and a golf course in the north. From this foundation, the sides of the triangle waver up inland, rising gently until the apex penetrates the chalk to admit a river, a railway line and an elegant military canal from the Martello period. Time has not so much stilled here as become its own subject. The modern conurbation hides a complex remnant known, wherever you come across its eighteenth century inns, manses and customs sheds, as Old Town – never 'the Old Town'. It's a heritage both compact and distributed. Halfway along the short edge of the triangle, the visitor will discover with delight the reconstructed pier, the arcades, the bohemian pubs packed out on open-mic night but on the verge of extinction the rest of the week, the fish and chip bars. Back from the sea, there are books and antiques, cakes and a delicatessen, one-stop open-water swimming shops serving the same clientele as the contemporary galleries and museums.

A trickle of through-traffic can still be expected at weekends, though A-roads inland appropriated most of it long before the present crisis. Gull cry presides over it all, immemorial, eerie, maudlin, yet rarely unexciting – the sound of dead pensioners mourning the great vanished battles of Britain.

On an overcast day in late summer, an older woman in a maroon woollen winter coat can be seen squatting in the road midway between the largest of the art galleries and the roundabout at the end of the coast road, wrestling with a home-made rectangular placard about three feet on its long edge. She has an air of encampment, nervous and purposeful one minute, smiling around delighted the next. Her French trail shoes are caked with mud. Her sign is presented sometimes at chest level, sometimes at the full extension of her arms above her head. It is like a sail, so hard to handle, skittish and kiting in the slightest breeze. Sometimes she offers it to the northbound lane, more often to the south, as if she's forty years younger and hitchhiking and the words HOW CAN YOU MISPLACE A CONTINENT? propose less a subject for debate than some reified metaphysical destination.

The sign

—

No cars enter the town that morning. Midday the old woman eats a home-made sandwich. Later, a cloud or two will gather high over the sea, while a breeze rustles the leaves of the exotic plantings on the roundabout. A family of holidaymakers consisting of two adults and three children will be seen walking up the beach and then down again. They stop, as if listening. At that, sounds as of an approaching petrol engine can be heard, aggressive downshifts at first distant then suddenly quite close, accompanied by the familiar backfires and clatters of a throttle bypass anti-lag. There's an instant of silence as the vehicle enters the roundabout. The old woman treads on the hem of her coat, totters to her feet and waves the sign above her head.

The vehicle that exits the roundabout is no longer a car.

In a complex frame of metal tubing, suspended on four huge tractor wheels, are cradled a long, old-fashioned aircraft engine wrapped round with copper pipes and bundles of electrical wiring; clusters of what seem to be household butane gas bottles; and, well to the rear, two padded seats from a military jet of the 1950s, into which are strapped a crew of two. From time to time, this machine seems to be enveloped by a radiant discharge. It accelerates and speeds towards her. As soon as she catches sight of it, she'll panic, drop her sign and flee first towards the sea then back towards her core territory, the museum.

This will happen through every iteration.

The sign

—

THE VEHICLE THAT EXITS THE roundabout is not a car. It is a complex space-frame suspended on four huge tractor wheels. It accelerates. It speeds towards her. Catching sight of it, she drops her sign, totters first towards the sea then away from it. The driver overcorrects to avoid her. Control is soon lost. The vehicle fishtails, banging repeatedly into the rails of the promenade, uprooting the memorial benches and throwing them about.

We see now that the driver is a wasted old man. His face runs the gamut of expression – fearful one moment, savage and excited the next. His long grey hair tangles in the slip-stream. His lips contort. He has fastened himself into a tight brown leather suit along the arms and legs of which run clusters of neoprene tubing. Out of these at intervals erupt thin coloured fluids, which splatter over his chest or into his eyes. Though he blinks furiously, he suffers no harm; but wherever the vehicle is touched, it blackens and smokes briefly. Lightning writhes along its chassis members.

One huge wheel flies off suddenly into the air! The pilot claps his hands to his face. In the same moment, the vehicle mounts the oceanside kerb and, briefly airborne, reaches the beach, where it slithers in circles. Gouts of shingle and water spray up until it stalls suddenly and rocks to a halt beneath the pier. Silence falls. The children of the beach family begin to cheer and dance. The smell of unburnt fuel drifts briefly inland.

The sign

—

In each subsequent iteration, the vehicle's crew of two seems to be attached to the machinery by thick but flexible hoses, although it will never be clear whether these connections are biological or electrical. It is not a car. We see now that the driver is a wasted old man. In an attempt to avoid the woman with the sign, who now darts this way and that in the road in a panic, he overcorrects and loses control. One of his machine's huge wheels detaches itself without warning, to bounce away towards the thirteenth green of the golf course at the north end of the promenade. The driver claps his hands to his face and claps his hands to his face. He claps his hands to his face.

As the vehicle jumps the oceanside kerb and slithers across the beach in front of the astonished holidaymakers – whose children at this point begin to shout and dance gleefully – it is enveloped by a radiant discharge, or St Elmo's fire, through which the crew can be seen helplessly or furiously waving their arms. Are they prisoners of the machine? Or do they enjoy life on the edge of disaster like this? Shingle sprays up from the remaining three wheels, until, beneath the rusty understructure of the pier, the vehicle scrapes itself to a halt. Silence now falls; the smell of unburnt fuel drifts briefly inland. The driver detaches himself from his machine and pulls off his leather helmet. His face looks indistinct.

'For god's sake, Marnie,' he calls wearily. 'Can't you ever, just for once, think what you're doing?'

Static phenomena

—

LATER, WHEN SHE QUESTIONED HIM about what had happened, Phillip didn't seem to understand. 'The car's OK,' he kept saying, as if that was what she'd asked. He rubbed his eyes and stared around the atrium. His skin seemed both illuminated and grey. He smelled strongly of smoke. One side of his face had a slightly swollen look, as if he had recently spent time too close to an open fire; by contrast, the other side seemed emaciated, stripped down. He was emphatic but anxious. 'Nothing like that happened,' he assured her. 'You can see the car, it's out there and it's just the same as ever.' But something had happened, she was perfectly convinced of that. She had been privy to events, she had seen what she had seen: she would see it again, she knew, were she to leave the gallery and stand patiently in the road holding up a sign. Could Phillip tell her what he had seen?

He was fine, he told her instead; he was fine and the car was fine. That was the main thing, surely. 'But, Marnie, I almost ran you over. You really mustn't sit in the *road* like that.' Then: 'Alice has gone. She sailed Tuesday.' He laughed. 'I mean yesterday,' he said. And then uncertainly: 'You remember Alice?'

'Of course I remember Alice,' Marnie said. 'Who could forget her? I'm not stupid.' She wanted to know more, she said. Of course she did. 'But, Phillip, where have you been?' His response was to offer her a thin leather-covered notebook smelling as if it had recently been dropped in a fire.

'I want you to read this.'

'Look,' she told him, 'you're welcome to stay with me in the gallery. There's plenty of room for both of us' – then, as he was opening his mouth to reply – 'but that thing will have to sleep in the car.'

Phillip passed his hands across his face.

'I'm holding together well, thanks,' he said. 'Thanks for asking.'

The size of an adult human being, and nothing like the object Phillip had originally brought to Marnie's door, the artefact still had an unformed look. Once you accepted that, it was easy to find yourself disturbed by the grace of its movements. It clasped Marnie's hands delightedly between its own, exclaiming, 'He's holding together well!'

Marnie pulled herself loose.

'I don't know what you're doing here and I don't want to.'

'No one knows what they're doing here,' Phillip said in a detached voice. He scratched his cheek.

The artefact followed him closely wherever he went, standing at his shoulder and staring up into his face like a lip-reader when he spoke. It never slept, but sat near him if he did, or else moved quietly between windows that gave a view of the sea, as if trying out different angles on the moonlit water. Marnie, who soon grew bored with them both, was left with the housekeeping. She queued at the minimarts tucked away on lines of economic stress where New Town interfaced with Old. She frequented a hot snacks van that traded irregularly from a viewpoint car park above the shingle line; since she could never predict its next appearance, she would buy two or three meals at a time and keep them in one of the cooler rooms. If you didn't hide food, the artefact would eat it immediately. It would eat anything, including cooked hamburger four days old. But of the food Marnie made, its favourite was cold tinned mackerel mashed and stirred into porridge.

The rest of the time she walked, allowing the concrete paths and slipways of the old sea defences to draw her out past the golf course. Lines of renovated cottages were still half occupied by people from the city trying to live their weekend lives. The cottages were easy to enter and a reliable source of paracetamol. Small birds flocked in the dense shrubbery of gardens run to seed. Not far behind the houses, low-lying rose-bushes and brambles crept cautiously inland to merge with elder and hawthorn on the slopes beneath the chalk cliffs. On wet days she was uneasy with herself, increasingly confused, but she found an obscure comfort in the abandoned gardens. On the seaward side, it was ragwort, escaped fuchsia and honeysuckle. Teasels, sea kale, patches of scrub and stabilised grassland with bramble and willow species.

'I found something like old man's beard?' she reported. 'But much smaller and creeping everywhere along the ground? Do you know the name of that?' Phillip only stared at her. 'You should really go for a walk,' she advised. 'It would be good for you. Neither of you ever go outside.'

Speedball oils

—

BEFORE ANY OF THIS BEGAN to happen, not long after she came out of the Slade, Marnie was still trying to paint her way against the tide.

She rented a studio in East London, and laid it out with matt white walls, a black futon pushed across a door she didn't use, two long shelves of books high up, the same line carried along the next wall by four small square canvasses. There were sometimes a couple of larger rectangular paintings on the walls, and several small ones stored on shelves where the chimney breast had been taken out. An overall hung on the back of the door. She always placed herself in the room, not along its edges; kept turpentine in an old inkwell. Would never use white spirit because she believed it was carcinogenic. 'Always have a lid on the bin for turpentine rags,' she would advise visitors, 'especially in a small room. Otherwise you have to live with the fumes.'

It was as if she believed they were painters too. They were already painters, just by being there and being interested. Brushes would always be laid out for them on the floor next to the glass palette, on ribbed or corrugated paper to stop them rolling about. There would be a tub of acrylic gesso primer, a wire filing basket chaotic with Speedball oils. Vandyke brown, Indian red, crumpled tubes leaden in the dull light. Oxide of chromium. Monestial green.

She would sit in the studio looking at the ghost of the light on the white wall, certain it had changed. In a shoe box she kept small sketches on French watercolour paper – wavering pencil lines and little dabs of paint, their edges torn neatly along a ruler. 'They're often the best of it,' she would say, hoping it was a clue to what she wanted. She grew adept with a Nikon, and often used her slide projector the way Canaletto used his camera obscura, to throw an image direct on to canvas.

Whenever Marnie remembers the studio, it's a shock, as if she's remembering it for the first time. She sees that the picture on the easel is unfinished. It's always different. Women and children caught at Columbia Road Market or in the next street across. Or a woman stares out at you and over her shoulder you see a sketchily imagined background of desks in a school. Whenever she thinks about the East London studio,

Marnie remembers two things: the unfinished picture on the easel, and Phillip's mother, who, on a rare visit, stared at it in a kind of aesthetic panic and said without warning, 'I don't want you and Phillip to meet again,' then, looking around at the other pictures, added dismissively, 'No one will be doing this soon.'

They quarrelled more often

—

SOON IT WAS POSSIBLE TO sit down daily on the kerb outside the gallery and hold up her sign without seeing anything more than flickers and brief changes of light across the shingle. If Phillip had somehow brought the bad patch with him, his arrival had also caused it to curl itself away into the astral plane. Light drizzle fell across the scenes of the old man and his vehicle, darkening and browning first the air and then the images themselves. Across a week, at first easily visible from the coast road, then elusive and dependent on the viewer's exact position with regard to the old pier, they faded, until all you could see was the shingle, the tracks of the ever-circling family, and above that, a dull uniform sky with a single horizontal breach revealing, quite a distance away to the north, some pillars of cumulus illuminated by the sun. One sky, she thought, a window on another. Meanwhile, the atrium was littered with signs.

They rested against the walls, or against each other, each one made with more care than you would expect – less like a placard than a primed canvas on a stretcher – though its legend, which remained the same, was as dashed-down as lipstick writing on a mirror. It was work that filled her with satisfaction; work, she believed, that elbowed out any other work she had done in her career. She stopped only now and then to drink a cup of black tea, listening to the rain on the windows or the sea wind around the curtain wall. HOW CAN YOU MISPLACE A CONTINENT: words that had tumbled through her head for half a decade before she could make anything of them. Like litter blowing down the coast road, useless and always renewed.

'Why are you doing this,' Phillip complained. 'Is this what you think art is now?' While the item, smiling shyly, stood and watched the two of them argue, whispering, 'I love what you do.' It fetched books at random from the theory shelf of the gift shop and lingered while Marnie pretended to read them.

'Do you know what?' it said. 'I think you've given us all permission.'

'What on earth are you talking about?'

Phillip wasn't well. He held his head slightly to one side when he looked at you and seemed always to be listening for something, a sign she recognised from the influenzas and

Covids of his childhood. His hands trembled, his right eye was slow to open in the mornings. Some days all he did was leaf irritably backwards and forwards through the notebook he had offered her, as though looking for a passage he remembered but couldn't find. Marnie had tried to read a page or two, but it turned out to be someone's journal of the invasion, rich with phrases like 'Long before the iGhetti arrived, everyone was playing out a separate fantasy' and 'The seas are like a stew, still full of the biological artefacts they discarded after their arrival.' It seemed ridiculous to her. The fact was, she tried to explain to him, that all she wanted to do now was her own work. It was so important to her! Since the crisis became permanent, she had found it hard to concentrate on anything that made her feel as if the life she was living wasn't hers.

'I don't want what's happening to be owned' – and by that, she said, she meant *described* or *explained* – 'by anyone else. I wonder if you can understand that? Do you feel anything like it?'

'Marnie, you've never been any other way.'

She recoiled from the sudden painful glitch or turn this brought about in her own view of herself; then, considering it as briefly as she could, concluded, 'I think you're being glib. And perhaps a little bitter.' Then added: 'I wonder why you only kept my side of the correspondence?'

'Which correspondence?'

'All our emails!' she said. 'Don't you remember our emails? You were such a nice boy!'

'Marnie, I'm thirty-eight years old.'

After that, as if preparing to confront on some unacknowledged level, express some deeper grievance or division, they quarrelled more often.

Some of the shops she frequented had tucked themselves away up in the long tail of the town. She was walking back one evening – the air warm and soft, the Military Canal bathed in rose-coloured light, even the gulls quiet – when the display window of an Oxfam caught her eye. The usual objects were on show, no one was in charge, but the door was open and inside at the back – among the unreadable novels, appalling ornaments and picked-over clothes rails – a familiar figure seemed to move, unfinished, uncertain, but curiously fluid.

Marnie went inside and said, 'Why are you in here?'

The artefact said it was looking for some nice things. 'What do you think of this,' it asked, 'with this? I'd love to know what you think.'

Marnie was reluctant to think anything at all.

After a moment, she admitted, 'I suppose you've got to wear something.'

'I'll just put them in a bag.'

'You should always be careful to leave the money, even if there's no one behind the till.'

'I love the shops,' the artefact said.

From then on, it could be seen around Old Town in an oversized men's jacket, and a white dress shirt worn outside rolled jeans. Its ankles were always bare, the sleeves of the jacket pushed up its forearms and the cuffs of the shirt folded back carefully over them. To this outfit, it might add a Varanasi scarf and ballet flats, then appear unexpectedly out of the holm oaks and looted public houses of Marnie's coast walks or sit down companionably beside her on the gallery steps while she held up her newest version of the sign. In addition, it had begun talking to itself in different voices during the night. 'A new life,' it announced, in the commanding tones of a four-year-old playing on its own in a garden, 'is *beginning*.' It had persuaded one of the fourth-floor exhibits to work, a boxy tube TV from the 1950s repurposed to show fragments of soft drink ads from the middle Thatcher period, in front of which it sat for hours, cross-legged and with a shy, inturned smile.

'It seems to want company,' Marnie suggested. Phillip only replied, 'I never encourage it.' The more energy the artefact displayed, the less he seemed to have. It was really quite noticeable.

None of them were sleeping well. At night, like exhibitions, they kept to separate spaces. Whatever time you woke, someone was always awake before you. The artefact watched the same ads over and over again in its fourth-floor annexe and never slept at all. The man sat on the floor halfway down a passage between two big rooms, his knees drawn up, leafing petulantly through some other man's notebook. The old woman, as she now thought of herself, saw all this. As darkness fell, she rested on her pile of Mondrian-adjacent soft goods and listened for the tide. Was it rising or falling? She watched for the moon through the tall and elegant atrium windows. Her teeth ached. Her hips ached. Uncompliant memory and dementia led her from one vague, brief, forgotten tranche of life to another, then back to a present that wasn't really anywhere at all.

Under these conditions, trying to remember who or where you are becomes too much of a nuisance: instead she wandered the building looking for the others. One night – under the impression she was in the Prado in 2006, though part of her knew full well she wasn't – she found them in the artefact's room. They'd arranged themselves in a tableau that featured the TV set and viewing bench. Phillip, standing, looked down at the artefact from behind, his hands on its shoulders. The artefact turned its head to look back and up at him, as if he had arrived only that minute. Very slowly, their faces were coming together, while the fluttering light of the TV screen threw a dual shadow on the wall. Catalogues from past exhibitions had heaped up around the base of the bench and drifted across the floor until they broke like a wave in the junction between two walls.

Though she said nothing, Marnie made it clear she had seen what was happening. She stood still, and, in what she later came to understand as a moment of pure catastrophe, they all three stared at one another with a kind of blank startlement. The jaw of Tennent's shadow – which had now grown huge, oblique and elongated – was beginning to extrude itself from the head, like the cartoon of a drawer opening. No one spoke a word. She would never find a way to describe the intensity of this engagement; it had no place in any emotional structure she acknowledged. There was, perhaps, an element you could only describe as 'diligence' – although you would always wonder what you meant by that. Marnie, suddenly desperate to confirm who she was, left as silently as she had come and hurried down the shallow stairs to find her tote, while Phillip, managing to disengage himself from the artefact, followed her into the atrium, calling in the voice of a spoiled ten-year-old:

'Marnie, what am I *supposed* to do?'

'I don't care,' Marnie said. 'I don't care!'

The artefact came and stood near the bottom of the stairs in a cloud of Givenchy's L'Interdit, with one hand on the bannister rail, watching them uncertainly. Every so often it descended another step. The atrium had begun to fill with predawn light and outside the seabirds were waking, if they had ever been asleep. The ocean was very flat. Marnie had found her bag and now began to fumble about inside it for the items she recognised.

'I don't care what you do,' she repeated.

He said: 'We don't know how to make best use of their stuff, only how to live a worse life of the kind we already had.'

He said: 'I hoped for a future but it just isn't here.'

He said: 'Marnie, I'm sailing. Tomorrow.'

'Why are you saying this?'

'Alice was right, there must be something else. Nobody in the rest of the world could have been this stupid. I'm taking the find with me. Someone out there might know what to do with it. I'll go down the coast tomorrow – the Gaufs will buy the car, they see it as an art object. And if you want to come, I'll get you a ticket. I'll get tickets for us all.'

'I don't know why you're saying this.'

'I'll get tickets for us all!'

The tote was fuller than she would have preferred – pulled out of shape like herself, she thought, by its contents. All the walking in the rain and then the shopping trips. It had never really been a bag to carry your luggage in. She had bought it, who could remember when, because she liked the logo. She could see her hand, still moving aimlessly about inside it beneath the grimy cotton, selecting and rejecting. Phillip seemed cheerful enough, if a little insistent. 'We can all go together!' she heard him repeat, as if he had made an amazing discovery. She managed to look away before the gun went off. When she opened her eyes again, he was sitting against the wall with his legs spread out and the top half of his body leaning to one side. The smell in the atrium was indescribable. She felt as if every part of her life was separating, segment from segment pulling apart like something sticky that you ate and weren't sure you liked. She held up the gun; turned it this way and that. Panic wouldn't help.

'What have you done to yourself this time?' she asked tiredly.

They waited all day to see if he would die. Night came, and every time a car murmured past in the dark, the artefact hurried to the window. Under moonlight, Phillip presented the drawn yet peaceful face of a bog burial, as if he had been killed but had got over it. His inflamed eyelid drooped. The fall had broken his elbow on the same side. Everything else, she tried not to see; everything either of them said seemed to travel a long way, like a message in another medium. The rolled and charred notebook stayed by his side. The charred notebook with the broken spine and the broken man: they remained with each other. Once or twice he plucked at it and the pages fluttered in the night's draughts. Marnie opened it and read to him at random, from entries that swung randomly between the personal and the historical. She had no idea who the writer was. One moment, he was telling you about the arrival of the iGhetti, the next he seemed to be writing about his family; then sometimes, in some way, about both at once –

*

May 17th: Perhaps I was too much for my parents, perhaps I made things too difficult. That was the feeling I had from my mother. That I made things too difficult for her. I was an embarrassment to her. She couldn't stand mess. She decorated often. Bought new furniture and carpets. She cleaned and cleaned. Even at that age, I could feel her looking around in a numb way and wondering how she would make sense of it all, which I don't think she ever did. Things were too much for her. I can't stand mess, she would tell me, meaning, I can't stand the mess you've made of my life. It wasn't that she had any other plans. For her it was just the day-to-day business of things being made more difficult, requiring more of an investment than she was able to give. 'What would you be,' she sometimes asked, 'if you could be one other thing?' and go on to claim that she wanted to be something outlandish. A coelacanth. A rhino. Why would anyone ask that? What purpose is there in a question like that?

August 2nd: In my confusion, ten years old, I dreamed suddenly of huge insects speaking to me through my mother, who, from then on, I called the Girl Beneath the Dragonfly. She had been thrown out of herself by their need to speak. She was a radio, she lay in regions of sodden black ash where they had switched her on. They stood over her, trembling. They were trying to explain how badly things had gone wrong. How they had been blown here by circumstances they could not control. How they didn't mean to be here. They had never been meant to be here, on Earth as we knew it then.

[Date illegible]: The world's over. But that doesn't matter. Because another one will be along soon enough.

Next morning, propped up and semi-conscious in the hot light of the empty atrium, Phillip stared intently south-east at a horizon line that was, from soon after dawn, almost obscured by a continual procession of mirages. Dense, stacked, towering, undecodable, these Fata Morgana had at one and the same time the qualities of being thoroughly suspect and obviously real. Of the two of them, she thought – although she couldn't think why – Phillip would be, from now on, the one with the advantage of age. His final action was to pull her close and whisper urgently, 'Marnie, we're none of us well.' It was dark again by then, and she could see distant lights to the south and east. 'Are you listening? Unless we can learn from them,' he said, 'we don't even know what we're seeing.' This was a plea, she understood. It was the real wound, bringing with it instant images of him as he made his *Wanderschaft* from beach community to beach community down the coast towards her in the immediate aftermath of the disaster. She didn't know how to attend to it. What had begun as his desire to see and understand the end of the world had decayed first into a kind of adventure sport, then a profession, and at the last, a burden. This struck her as one of the inevitable trajectories of anxiety.

He shouted: 'They took everything and we got this junk in return.'

'Maintaining your expectations is one thing,' she said, as if he was fifteen years old. 'It's altogether another thing to be so easily thrown.'

'No! No!'

She put her arms around him and rocked him until he was silent.

'Goodbye, Phillip,' she said.

The artefact knelt down and touched the dead man's shoulder. Then it stood up and hugged Marnie. 'Anyone can be hurt,' it concluded, 'and we often do unpredictable things because of it. I'm sorry for your loss.'

'This is all your fault. You can help me get him out of here.'

'He looked so tired,' it said.

Land of lost content

—

EVEN THE MOST ESTABLISHED BEACHCOMBING location will lose its charm quite suddenly. All it requires is a certain nervousness to arise among the beachcombers themselves. Inexplicable losses of optimism spread in quiet concentric circles like the graphic representation of radio waves on the cover of a 1920s popular science magazine. One night the shingle is a winding avenue of lights, visible from a hundred and twenty miles up; the next, the laughter has departed, the impromptu garlands and threesomes are gently but firmly shredded, the guitars and old tunes have gone quiet. The wrong things are coming out of the ocean. There has been a subtle loss of confidence; a change of fortune does the rounds, no one's dream is mapping on to the market any more – if, they decide, it ever did. In a day or two the shoreline will be deserted.

North of the museum, the other side of the pier and all along the ocean side of the golf course, a similar loss of faith – perhaps even the first of its kind – had taken place a year or so after the catastrophe. A handful of benders – decked out with blanched strips of cloth, faded ribbons and the flex from solar fairy lights – stood intact but skeletonised by the sea wind, surrounded by the scattered remains of the original colony, a lot of stumps that curved up out of the shingle like the ribs of small boats or large fish. Here and there lay the remains of some large object that had actually washed in from the sea, dead before or after butchering, its bones – if that's what they were – still articulated at angles that only led your gaze towards puzzlement and private anxiety. Everything tapped and creaked on a rising onshore wind.

Into this failed attempt to reframe the disaster, two figures now dragged a third. Their efforts, though in no way brutal, were efficient enough. Its heels left a winding accusatory track, one end of which singled out the moonlit doors of the art museum. 'Leave him here,' Marnie said. 'This is far enough.' She went from one bothy to another looking for something to use as an urn until she found a metal biscuit tin she thought would do. Then she changed her mind and they retraced their steps a little, so they could set fire to Phillip beneath the pier, right where it met the sea on a thin strip of sand that revealed itself only around low tide.

'Hurry,' she told the artefact, 'and collect wood. Plastic. Anything we can burn. Be quick!'

She threw the notebook in on top of him, and for an hour or two trudged back and forth between the museum and the bonfire, her arms full of painted canvas, half-finished protest signs and volumes of contemporary theory. The flames went up high and energetic. Ash and sparks whirled around in the columns and billows of heated air, indistinguishable from one another. Marnie watched them streak and float across the corner of her visual field, struggling against the realisation that they were, by some more or less intimate connection, Phillip. The smell was hard to avoid, but she managed. By dawn things had cooled down and she could scrape up enough of the ashes to half fill the biscuit box, unsure in the end what was driftwood and what was unburnt bone.

The artefact had gazed earnestly out to sea while all this was happening, then danced suddenly around the flames and later the embers, waving its arms. She wasn't sure what it might be feeling, if it ever felt anything.

'Get in the car,' she told it, 'and don't be silly.'

When they had both settled down, she started the car and sat there for some time, touching the wheel, or leaning forward as if she had seen something stuck on the windscreen.

'I can't do this,' she said eventually. 'I don't know why I thought I could do this.' The artefact smiled and offered her the notebook, a bit more charred but still intact; its hand, she saw, was a little charred too. It was already busy healing itself. 'Christ,' she said. 'You moron.' She switched off the engine, got out, slammed the door, and walked down the beach past the embers of the fire. She stood close to the water staring out at the lost continent. A little later, the artefact came up close behind her, and she heard it say:

'I can drive. I'd so love to drive that special car of his.'

When she didn't answer, it added: 'You won't have to worry.'

PART TWO:

Marnie's Holiday

—

Forgotten coast

—

A VEHICLE IS SEEN COMING down off the chalk and into a town, in powerful unchanging afternoon sunlight. Establishing shots reveal a country with the qualities of a 'wrong' UK. A hot glare comes up off the sea, and along here, every other little port seems to advertise itself as 'the balcony of the lost continent', which can only really be interpreted to mean: 'the balcony from which a lost continent might be seen'. Each morning of the endless summer, chairs are arranged in the breakfast rooms and on the terraces of the old-fashioned hotels, cleverly but sympathetically refurbished so that the groups of tourists – of which there are many may stare out to sea with their early coffee and croissant, as if dawn were an exotic form of sunset, some vast, gorgeous, fragile – though thoroughly dependable – glitch in the real.

Marnie now thinks of the artefact as 'the driver' and doesn't know how it occupies itself when they aren't in motion. When they are, though, its attention remains firmly on the road and its hands firmly on the wheel; it is a mine of information about the things they see.

'The administrative divisions of this coast,' it tells her, 'were for a long time called "lathes". But no one knows what language that word came from.' Or: 'That's quite a nice little cafe to stop at if you get tired. You can sit there and have a coffee.' Marnie, dazzled and lulled by the sunshine, has looked out too late to catch the latter; and anyway, how could it know? It doesn't seem to her as if an organism that emerged so recently from the sea can possibly be an authority on anything.

Marnie has her good days and her bad days. She finds it increasingly hard to leave a room. She will shut the door and then go back again immediately and open it and shut it again to make sure, and then get in the car and struggle back out of it and go back inside to be certain she has shut the door again. When she has finally settled in the passenger seat, she sometimes won't leave it at the other end of the journey. She knows she's being mulish but she can't stop. The miles unravel smoothly for all that. The driver is so patient! Its hands are strongly formed now, as if at last it has finished arriving from the sea. They are well delineated, with almond-shaped nails that have a carefully tended look and are often done in startling colours, pearly and metallic at the same time, emitting the faintly perceptible inner glow of plastic.

The Peppermint Bay Hotel

THE THING ABOUT A LARGE room, Marnie thought, is that sunshine falls aslant from the bay windows into unpredictable corners – where the strings of fairy lights are still blinking on and off from the night before – so you can always find somewhere cool to sit in the morning.

She had finished her croissant and was listening to the two women at the table next to hers continuing an argument begun somewhere else. That morning they had chosen brand variations on the same outfit: billed cap over a ponytail drawn preternaturally tight, with a thin lozenge-quilted gilet and compression tights. Now they pushed back their chairs from the ruins of breakfast to give themselves room, and one of them kept demanding, 'Look at me now! Look at me now!', accompanying this with a movement of her shoulders to indicate self-disgust. 'I've only been up for an hour and look at me! This is how I am!' No reply. 'Yeah, well, I feel crap now. Thanks for that. No, really. Thanks for that.'

After a few minutes, a child of about six years old joined them and stood there silently, as if wanting to contribute but not being sure how. Something about his caution and generosity, the way he already understood how to give them space, made Marnie feel calm, but sorry too. She found her tote, held it up to catch his attention and said, 'I've got something here you might like. Close your eyes and hold out your hands.' The child assessed her cautiously. He took a step or two towards her, stared back at the women, then up again at Marnie, then out of one of the big bay windows, blinking in the glare off the sea.

'Come on,' she encouraged. 'Pretend it's Christmas!'

He smiled suddenly and cupped his hands; into them, after some scraping about, she measured a few golden snowflakes from the bottom of her bag. Then a few more. An embarrassingly strong smell of the tideline – mud and salt and something dead – came out of the bag with them and filled the room like a fart. One of the women leaned over and said, 'Excuse me? Are you staying here?'

'Christmas!' Marnie replied, with her best smile. 'I used to love it when I was his age, didn't you?'

At his age, everything about that season had seemed mysterious to her, holding its breath, quivering on the edge of change. Whatever point of the year you viewed it from, you could already see Christmas as a place of promise, an enchanted island rising from nowhere in the winter dark, illuminated by tiny lights in rich deep blues and reds, the very opposite of the climate on that forgotten coast. She had watched the same happen to Phillip, then, after a year or two, pass.

'Of course, I don't suppose any of us knows quite what season it is now.'

Back in their room, she found the driver sitting with the curtains drawn, occupied with a pack of ordinary playing cards, dealing them face up into unequal piles by some system she couldn't understand, then sighing and quickly folding them together again.

'I'm tired of this,' it said. 'Could you help?'

'It's no good asking me,' said Marnie, who had always loathed games. She pulled the curtains apart so that light flooded across the complicated clothes and naive, entitled expressions of the kings and queens.

'There,' she said. 'See if that helps.'

'Where did I come from?' the driver said. 'Do you know?'

Later she caught it looking into the old-fashioned wardrobe mirror, whispering to itself, turning its head from one side to the other as if trying to surprise some reflection in the corner of its own eyes. At night, it would leave the hotel and wander about the town, returning only to leave again immediately.

From these quiet, opaque forays, it brought back a chess set missing one white pawn; dried flowers and tampons; a man's shirt – cool on the skin, very clean and old. The smaller items were always laid out for Marnie on her bedside table, in careful arrangements that changed daily. She couldn't help interpreting them as language, but if she asked, 'Why have you brought me this?' or 'Which part of your life do these things come from?', it would only look confused for a moment then carry on doing whatever it had been doing. It would have liked to answer, she thought, but there was a check between what it understood about itself and what it wanted Marnie to understand. Sometimes, on return, its clothes would be damp. It had learned to read in a day, and often practised by quoting from the ads in the thriving local freesheets. 'The sky's the limit,' it exclaimed, 'for Rhino Roofing!' And: 'Elephant House Ice Cream!'

The shirt was voluminous and came down to Marnie's knees; paradoxically, its collar proved too tight to fasten.

Three o'clock in the afternoon, they struggled up the steep and wandering path to the top of the headland on the north side of the bay. There the chalk swept down to the sea like an arm in a green medieval sleeve, the cliff at the end a hand clenched round something you might sense but never see. Though it would be light for an hour or two yet, the wind had already begun its nightly turn onshore; at the top of the cliff, the air proved blustery, the footing undependable. Viewed from up there, the cove lay undecided about itself or its offer to the passing trade. For Marnie, transporting Phillip in his biscuit box – its well-fitting lid featuring UK royals down the ages dressed in uniforms of their own design – this was just one more small disappointment in a growing succession of them.

'It wouldn't be quite the right place for him,' she told the driver, meaning that it wouldn't be right at all. And then: 'Are you listening?' But, excited by the weather, it was taking the downward path at a run, flailing its arms comically above its head as if in free fall. She had to laugh. 'You aren't listening in the slightest!' she shouted into the wind, and followed more carefully, holding the makeshift urn in front of her as if offering it to someone.

Below them spread the beach: first shallowly, then steeply sloped; pebbles patched with open sand, rimmed with weeds and rubbish, evening primrose, sparse sea buckthorn, the trickle of a sewer outflow, an abandoned ice cream parlour. It was empty but for two women trying to persuade their little boy to go in the sea, where a small boat could be seen from time to time – inflatable, dirty orange from long use, rolling precariously in the swell thirty yards offshore then obscured again as it fell into a trough between waves. Engine noise came and went, along with the faint, agitated shouts of the crew and their already appreciable complement of passengers. The child struggled, then allowed itself to be carried. It seemed desperate not to touch the water. By the time Marnie got down, the two women were up to their waists in the surf.

'What on earth are you doing?' she called. 'Where are you going? Can't you see he's afraid of what's in there?'

No reply.

The women waded, the boat waited, ugly and wallowing; the water's surface lost its polish, shifting from blue to grey over unexpected colours beneath. The entire episode folded itself away and was removed without conclusion, out to sea and out of sight. Nine o'clock in the evening, in an empty restaurant down by the harbour, she told the driver, 'I don't know what they must have made of me.'

'Try this food,' it said. 'You might not have eaten this before.'

'Don't be ridiculous,' Marnie said. 'It's haddock and chips.'

And then, surprising herself somehow: 'I'm not feeling entirely well at the moment. You can have mine.'

She wasn't sure how to describe what she felt. The events on the beach had spoiled her appetite; at the same time, whatever she was feeling had been there for a good part of her life, awaiting an excuse to reveal itself.

'Even if those women had wanted to hear me,' she said, 'the ocean would have drowned me out.' The moment she heard herself use the word 'drowned', she regretted it. The boat had kept rolling into view, its bow tilted almost vertical into the black air, then appearing to sink. The women had struggled through the water. 'By the time they were forced to swim, I couldn't see the child at all.' She imagined the women pushing it awkwardly ahead of them through the surf, like an improvised flotation aid. In a sense, she tried to explain, she didn't feel the child had ever been in their care. 'Not this morning, not this afternoon.' Rather, they had used it to keep themselves afloat.

'And where did they think they were *going*?' she asked, although she knew full well.

She took herself to bed but didn't sleep. She could hear the wind out there, shushing then blustering, far then almost immediately near, easily extricable from the voice of the tide. At 3 a.m. there came a prolonged musical grinding sound. It was the sound of something trying to drag itself ashore, up the shingle, past the tideline. Or it was only the transmission of a vehicle crossing the river from north to south in the distance. Why are we here? she asked herself. Why are we here? She wasn't referring to herself, or the artefact, or the dead Phillip, or the tourists. It was, she thought, a more general query than that. She felt better in the morning. Perhaps a little more tired than usual.

The possibilities of the space

—

DURING THE DAY, THE LIGHT burns down evenly, as if high summer never finished. They are travelling north, towards London, so the land is generally on the right, the sea on the left, but sometimes things are complex. Little inlets lead to long wooded detours. The road winds, widens and narrows. It bridges a stream in dappled shade; moves inland, following a contour; moves back towards the sea. Sometimes it seems to have reversed their direction of travel entirely. When she suggests this, the driver only laughs and, taking its hands briefly off the wheel, waggles its strong fingers. 'Jazz hands,' it says. 'Jazz hands!' Sometimes Marnie – who still feels a little distanced from things, a bit feverish, not entirely herself – becomes confused and believes she is retracing Phillip's journey south, or that, now he's dead, she actually is Phillip in some way.

Devoret St Michael, Preens Eddy, God's Heath, the road signs stand perfectly authentic at the sides of the road. Marnie doesn't recognise any of these names, but in the evening there is always another balcony town satisfyingly like and unlike the last: a cove and a hotel overlooking a square, with tables outside and a dinner jazz trio on a makeshift stage playing Frank Sinatra greats. (It seems impossible that they have called themselves 'Vinegar Rain', but perhaps something like it.) This makes a change from the traditional saudade performers, who specialise in songs which seem to be claiming 'I'm no longer angry and bitter', delivered in a voice which indicates a complete lack of self-knowledge. A man is making a phone call behind the stage. A black cat slinks past him, while women begin to dance and a boy briefly does a few simple tricks on a BMX, which no one notices, before he disappears up one of the steep streets to the left of the square. There is a light show. A little dry ice is emitted, but too soon smokes away. Coloured worms of light crawl across the stage, the backdrop, the building behind. They pass across the faces of the band and briefly fill the square, tentative but beautiful. From above, an estate agent's sign signals 'Country Properties' into the soft warm Kentish night. A smell of garlic prawns drifts temporarily across the cobbles. The women dance on. The children seek attention from their fathers, those style-conscious but dated men with shoulder bags, whose pinstriped short-sleeve shirts are worn outside tight denim shorts rolled and pressed a careful inch above the knee. The black cat now sits on the church steps, uncertain of its next move.

Sugar-free jelly

—

NEXT MORNING, IN THE DRY heat and neat white architecture of the town square, a mixed party of visitors in late middle age sat with their first cold beers of the day outside Cafe Optica, discussing the evolution of the condom since WWII. The Optica had no inside accommodation, just a stand-up bar in a narrow darkened space and four or five white tables under an orange awning on the pavement outside. The view from there led the eye down a steep little lane to a predictably dazzling vee of sea. At around eight in the evening, more tables would be added as needed – their clean cloths and candles in jars floating out white and luminous towards the centre of the square – and Optica would become a seafood place like all the others.

'You used to get them in every shape and size – no, really – I mean, for instance, with a cockerel's head on top.'

While each tourist contemplated a personal version of this absurd but somehow thought-provoking image, a five-hundredweight van pulled up a little way along the pavement. A workman got out at the front, hammered on the side of the van with the heel of his fist, and when nothing happened, shouted cheerfully in the local dialect. He began to slide ladders off its roof. Eventually the rear door of the van was flung open from inside and a second man emerged, yawning. He looked around as if he had expected to be somewhere else, then took hold of the nearest ladder, swung it across the pavement and leaned it almost tenderly against the wall of the cafe, so that the first man could climb it carrying another ladder balanced on his shoulder. Up they went confidently into the dry salt air and blinding light. The ladders rattled in the wind; without speaking a word, the men vanished over some railings and on to the Optica terrace. The visitors watched until there was nothing left to see. Then one of them said:

'You can get the Greek ones here.'

Shouts of laughter greeted this. 'No!' she insisted. 'Greek ones! At the pharmacy, you can! You *can*!'

They weren't sure what to do when a short older woman with shaggy grey hair and spectacles, wearing a paint splattered hiking waterproof and black jogging bottoms, approached their table and, taking a gun out of her shapeless cotton tote, asked, 'Look, sorry to interrupt. I wonder if you could advise me on something? Would that be all right? What do you think I should do with this?'

The truth was, they didn't know what to make of her. The pistol seemed real enough. They didn't know whether she was threatening them or trying to sell it. Or if the whole event – the men, the ladders, the gun, even the funny condom memories – was a figment, the remnants of some bad patch; at any rate, something very much in the style you would expect of a meeting on the King Henry VIII Balcony Trail in the world as they now knew it. A bad patch is what you make of it, and those south-east culture towns are all the same at noon. They already knew they must keep to the safe streets. Eventually someone said: 'I had my sugar-free jelly last night,' to further shouts of laughter. The old woman considered them for a minute or two, then let the gun drop back into her bag and wandered off, a little unsteadily, on the arm of her unformed-looking but rather beautiful companion.

The auberge

—

Eventually, though they still hadn't found a place where Marnie could feel comfortable scattering the ashes, they came to rest at a cluster of honey-coloured sandstone buildings in a narrow wooded fold of land half a mile from the sea. How long ago had it ceased to be a farm and made the move into hospitality? Accounts varied, with some more credible than others. The walls were thick. Inside, the rooms were small and comfortable, with low ceilings and uneven old plaster which browned any light that fell on it. There was furniture to match, vast dark wardrobes and dressers. There were smells of cooking, old and new. Lights twinkled off the bottles behind the bar downstairs, but it was less a pub, its customers agreed, than somewhere that looked after you and cooked well. That was the definition, after all, of an inn. Recent management changes had seen it renamed for one of England's most popular uncanonised saints: Edward the Confessor, patron of difficult marriages. As a result of these changes, one end of the main building – hidden during the heyday of the 1930s roadhouse trade behind the usual Tudorbethan facade – was still undergoing a sympathetic restoration to its original sixteenth-century glory.

'The scaffolding rather spoils things,' she told the driver.

'In fact,' it replied, 'the contemporary scaffolding has more in common with the building's actual past than this attempt to restore it, because rather than injecting its own values into the project, it is engaging directly with the same simple engineering problem the past had.'

'What are you talking about.'

'Your present day, like ours, is always-already vanishing. No history will be left at this site. Only heritage – an interpretation of the past as much an act of theft as the appropriation of another culture's artefacts and customs.'

'I suppose you think that's clever,' Marnie said, laughing out loud at herself. 'Who is "ours", anyway? Every day you get more like him. Do you know that?' But the driver had turned away and was staring inland, head tilted as if it had heard something.

'What do you mean by "ours"?' she insisted.

Their room at the Auberge St Edward was small yet comfortable. En suite, with a floor of dark, wide, ancient boards, the high polish of which reflected all the light from a casement window. They were looked after there by a girl you often saw behind the bar, or going in and out of the kitchen. That first afternoon she brought them a fruit that tasted like slightly sweetened rubber, half of which Marnie ate slowly, keeping away the many small flies with one hand. She wasn't sure she liked it. The girl watched Marnie carefully, her expressions changing as if she was eating it herself.

'Yum,' she said. And: 'We plant them every year, so they come up.'

This seemed too literal to mean anything. Why else would you plant anything, if not for it to come up? So instead of trying to answer, Marnie looked out of the window to where an old man, balanced precariously on a little rusty garden tractor – really, not much more than a toy – was turning the soil of the short sloping field below the house. His arms were sunburnt, his knees stuck out awkwardly, he seemed to be too frail to be working like that. He had with him a long dog, patched brindle and grey. The field seemed too small to be useful for anything. A hot light slanted in over the trees, and the dog ran about under it, untiringly, up and down the shallow furrows that were dark with moisture to begin with but dried out in minutes; it stopped at the end of each completed furrow to stand and stare around as alertly as if it had never stood in that field before. Its eyes were too emotionally guileless, too open and easily wounded for its own good.

After the girl had gone, taking the rind of the fruit away with her, Marnie said: 'So. "Come up". What's that? I thought she must mean something else.'

The driver seemed puzzled.

'"Come up"? Why, what it sounds like, of coursc. To grow. Marnie, what else could it mean?'

'Do you miss hearing the sea?'

The day after she ate the fruit, Marnie woke late, lay in bed for a few minutes feeling tired and disconnected, then threw up. The room was full of headache light reflected from the woods – green and amber at the same time. The driver was gone. She had no idea where it spent its nights. When it returned, she said, 'Today we should try inland. Somewhere with a view.' Not far from the auberge, the land flattened into a broad corridor of unfenced acid heath, dotted with villages of old brick, lapboard siding and lattice windows, where the sun struck off the windscreens of SUVs crowding around the village pond, just as they had every Saturday morning before they were abandoned. Out between villages, the road rose and fell in a series of inexplicable switchbacks through baked gorse and mats of dehydrating heather dissected by footpaths that swooped from whitened hardpack to black poached valley mud. Every horizon had its oast house. Everything was placed squarely, in light as solid as optical plastic.

*

All morning, she felt increasingly frail, as if something big was soon going to happen to her. Everything around seemed empty of life. It made her feel as though, if she were not careful, she would open her mouth, gape, and some unassuming liquid would pour out. The liquid would contain something which was her, but much that was not. No boundaries would be transgressed by this vomit. It would be almost cultural – more cultural, anyway, than physical. It would herald both a scalar change and an acceptable statement in some culture to which the driver had once belonged, or which it had represented, or served, or serviced.

'Let me out quickly,' she said, and knelt patiently by the side of the road among the rubbish and the dead grass until the spasm passed, thinking that while you can escape the major illnesses all your life, it's undeniable that something is going to happen to you in the end. Apart from the teeth, she hadn't done badly. Later, she sat up in the passenger seat with Phillip in his box on her knee and said, 'You don't even see much roadkill here.' Anything you saw on those lines was likely to be a faded burger package skittering across the road in the hot light – something that misled you but only for a moment.

'Maybe the wildlife is all dead,' the driver suggested. It laughed.

A few miles east, acid soils gave way to open pasture then wooded hills like intimate islands. A wind sprang up; lightning flickered beneath a sudden roll of cloud that blackened and liquified the heath. The driver raced back towards the sea and the auberge, where it helped her out of the vehicle then supported her across the forecourt through the cold teeming rain and she heard herself enquire after some time and a great distance had passed: 'Am I in a coma?' But, no, she would be fine, it reassured her as they reached the door of the inn at last. 'You'll be fine. You won't have to worry.'

Friends from the sea

—

CLEARLY, WHATEVER WAS HAPPENING INSIDE her had taken another turn. Fevers came and went; she kept Phillip's box and her FILBA tote close by her, to touch when time stretched and contracted. She was a trespasser on illness's estate now, wary, keeping a lookout, never sure if each new aspect or vista was a bad patch or dream. An uncertain watchfulness was sometimes the best she could manage. She wasn't entirely sure, any more, how to be ill: everything like that had happened long ago in her life. She had since learned how to rub along; how, in the absence of actual illnesses, to manage a steady decline. The business of the inn went on around her regardless. The girl came to bathe her, or bring more fruit that Marnie couldn't eat, though it presented, like the shower soap, in different sizes and the attractive, widely varying colours of peak Franz Marc.

Outside the room, meanwhile, the old man and his tractor ground up and down the little sloping field, reducing its dark earth to a finer and finer tilth while the dog trotted ahead all day in the green and amber light that slanted in over the woods. Nothing was ever planted; or so it seemed. Nothing changed. The long-dead Edward had her in his care: in fact, everything that happened in this space not only belonged to the saint but in some intriguing way *was* him, from the regular mealtimes to the warm, ready waters in the en suite to the nightly comings and goings of the driver.

She would wake dry-mouthed to its murmured discourse, finding it quite close to the bed, in the middle of distributing a basketful of objects, whispering to itself conscientiously, as in, 'Yes? No. No, no; not right.'

It brought back: cheap tickets, all colours; a bruised cricket ball, seams worn; a porcelain globe five inches in diameter bearing complex designs of leaves and tendrils in an approximation of delft blue; a small chest of drawers, veneered; a bicycle tyre; a National Insurance card and a gentleman's silver cigarette case: all gravityless, submerged-looking, warped by diffraction and wreathed in Christmas lights like strands of weed. It brought back a set of faded old china cups and saucers with a silver rim and a rose motif so worn you seemed to be seeing it through a mist. Arranging these gifts like objects in a shop window, it smiled down at her and left again, as if it had known all along she would sleep and forget. Illness made these night-time absences easier to endure, although not, perhaps, to understand –

As soon as the driver left the room, she believed, it took on a form taller and thinner than the entity she knew, and – dressed in a short black cotton work jacket buttoned tightly to the throat, black jeans a little too above the ankle, and old black boots on bare white feet – passed with a kind of swaying gait along the cobbled Old Town streets in the moonlight, up and down steep hills and flights of damp eroded steps towards the sea. It was always smiling around. It was pleased at everything. With quick, intuitive movements, it broke into this or that abandoned business, emerging not long after with its arms full.

Ten minutes later those same arms would have emptied again, as if it had decided none of that stuff was worth the effort. No action the driver performed could ever be described as furtive. It was always nodding companionably to shadows – not unlike itself but invisible to others – invisible perhaps even to each other. These parasites or helpers followed on behind. They had an elusive quality; only when they congregated, to stare up at an empty wall in an empty building by the Military Canal, could they be said to have a solid presence. Lounging about – awkward, unformed, dressed in equally strange clothes – they gave rise to a small but startling revelation every time they moved, as if emitting sparks, or a kind of music, while replicating the mechanical styles of the organ grinder's monkey.

But more often they simply stood still and stared up as if in admiration into the corners of the ruined rooms, while the driver watched them in its possessive, open-hearted way. Morning came on, and they all looked out expectantly over the sea. By then, everyone – including the girl from the Auberge St Edward, who now resembled child star Shirley Temple, complete with her fifty-six blonde curls, seen in one of her most iconic poses, vacationing by the pool at the Desert Inn, 1938 – had collected an object from the town, which they added ritualistically to a heap on the shingle.

'Take the stuff!' they encouraged the driver. 'We don't need this type of thing! Take it, she'll die for it!', before they waded back into the gentle waves.

Marnie woke, slept, woke again. The driver fetched stones and common seashells; a branch of forsythia photographed flowering out of season in a West London street; children's things made of feathers and cheap plastic, objects trivial in their day but now of great value to collectors. It fetched three blister packs of diazepam, use-by date too bleached to read. It offered her a Gisela Graham ceramic crab-themed mug.

'Why must you always do this?' she whispered. 'Where do you go to, when you meet your friends from the sea?' Turning to close the door on these occasions, it would smile more to itself than her, as if it found that question as difficult as Marnie did; only to pop back without warning a moment later carrying a collection of ancient letters, their dusty unopened envelopes paled or darkened in startling Cubism-inflected wedges where they had piled up across one another in some sunlit deserted hall.

'What are you really?' she whispered. 'And what do you think of us?'

She dreamed she had lost her bag. It seemed to her that she heard herself pleading, 'Why do you do this?'; and then, after some time, 'Am I already dead? I mustn't lose my bag!'

One week went by, and then another. Recovery was slow. Her appetite returned and she ate everything she was given. It was all fruit. It was all good nourishment. She could sit up in bed during the day. She could shower on her own. But despite a better night's sleep in general – despite two or three good nights' sleep in a row – she often felt tired by eight in the evening, and in her confusion still prone to hallucinate an imaginary town spreading itself outside the window, or a bat unfurling among the folds at the top of the curtains. Fireflies gathered near the ceiling, and a voice she couldn't identify but which she had grown to love would comment on the intimate events of her early life in a matter-of-fact whisper. Nevertheless, she felt so happy. Never anxious or afraid; only warm and tired and wrapped safely in the deep eros of the inn.

The murmuration

—

HER FIRST OUTING TOOK PLACE on the arm of the girl. It was warm, the girl said, and so she shouldn't have anxiety. 'I'm not having anxiety,' Marnie said, 'really I'm not.' They stood at the edge of the field and admired the sun-baked furrows. The dog watched them companionably, then turned to the old man on the tractor and barked once. They watched the sunset pour in over the ragged top of the woods for a moment or two – as if it was rising, Marnie said, not setting. A few mornings later, she saw Phillip's car pulled up close to the main door with its motor running. The driver rolled down its side window.

'It's a beautiful day!' it called. 'Let's go for a drive!'

She felt ambushed. 'Wait!' she said. 'Just wait, I must fetch Phillip!'

She had to admit she was glad to be out again. Sun after rain. Sodden heaps of earth in the fields. Birds beating southwards against a blustery wind. Mist blowing across the hilltop copses, threadbare pine trees on exposed slopes. A mass of chamomile. Orange poppies in the tall brown grass. She felt like gathering a whole armful of poppies, sweeping them up, wet and hairy-stemmed, petals already beginning to fall. Her arms would be covered with wet petals. She thought of orange petals floating on a dark green stream in some pre-Raph daub, and for once shivered with pleasure.

That day – her last day as what she could think of as herself – went by so quickly. Too soon it was the hour of soft warm light just before dinner, when the tourists take their drinks on to the balcony so they can sit and watch the ghosts of old men drawn out to sea, released from the mysterious dawn-to-dusk confinement of their commemorative benches along the north shore, to rise until they face out towards the lost continent. They arrive in ones and twos at first, unsteady-looking, balancing infirmly in the air, then suddenly there are hundreds, perhaps thousands of them rising from the warped, mouldy slats and mysteriously folded ironwork of all the other benches in all the other towns of the Henry the Eighth Heritage Trail, and they're driven out to sea until they've lost all individuality and they go wheeling through the characteristic yet unpredictable swings, the sudden folds and recursive figures of the murmuration; driven less like dead leaves on an offshore wind than – what? Marnie couldn't imagine the necessary set of rules. Instead, she stood and waved them off.

'Goodbye, Frank Horn! Goodbye, Bill Putnam!' she called. 'Goodbye!'

It was goodbye to Arthur; goodbye to Simon. Goodbye to Bert Lee, Samuel Albert, Albert Curry, Lee Shaw, Bill Shore and Dancey Smith (1928–2003). Goodbye to Jack Bunting and his brother Bareham, Everest Wilmington Hutton and Dennis Arthur Grant (1953). A fond farewell to Alan Whorlow, Emeritus Professor of Engineering, who loved to read about ships by the sea. Goodbye to Beech Mitchell and his treasured memories; Monty and David, inseparable and always in our hearts. Martin Shuttleworth from all his many, many friends: goodbye!

'Why are their wives never with them?' she asked the driver. 'Have you noticed? Their wives are never with them. What happens to the wives?'

They ate under a low moon, the light from which glistened on the cobbles around their table. It was their last meal together. A band of fog lay out to sea. Marnie touched the plates, the tablecloth; she moved the condiments about in their tall white containers like chess pieces modelled from de Chirico women. She looked down at her meal. Attentive as ever, the driver said, 'I love the little spines of the fishes, don't you?' Though prepared to be enchanted by this otherworldly viewpoint, Marnie saw just charred tails, white flesh, filmy bones like the fossil imprint of a leaf. Across the square, the band was setting up: The Local Favourites, on drums, Epiphone bass and electric piano.

'Isn't it trout?' she said uncertainly. 'I thought it was trout.'

Later she sat cocooned in the warmth of the car while the road rushed past and the driver told her about the stars. Its overwhelmingly boyish enthusiasms often made her think. Now she stared at its profile in the blue light of the dashboard – cut with white headlamp backwash that came on, corner to corner, in sudden flares and fades in time with the engine sounds, and saw once again that it was an artefact from the sea. No one knew what those things were supposed to do, or how they viewed a real person like her. The strangest quality of its face, she understood, was that it bore such a resemblance to the one she held in her memory, Phillip's face caught at the exact point between childhood and adolescence, at its most beautiful and unearthly.

'I feel as if he's with us here, too,' it said. It stared ahead, sighed, then leaned over suddenly and tapped the lid of Phillip's box. 'I know what you have in there. I feel as if he's with us here, in the special car he loved. Now more than ever!'

'Really, what do you think you are? What are you supposed to be?'

'We're always here to help.'

'But what do you think you *are*?' she insisted. And when

it only smiled, staring ahead into the white light and sudden curves: 'Take me home, then. You aren't him.'

Waking in the middle of the night, she went to the window. Outside, the little tractor continued to struggle up and down the furrows. It turned the newly turned-up earth again; it turned up stones, with little clicks and rattles. A new smell came up from the field on a warm breeze. The tractor was out there every night, sometimes with lights, sometimes without: you could never tell if the old man was aboard it or not. At night you never saw the dog. Even with the moon up like this, nothing much could be made out in the shadow of the woods.

You aren't him

—

When she turned back to the room, she saw for the first time that a tall armoire had been positioned diagonally across one corner. It was made of a black wood as hard as metal, originally decorated with carved lizards, complex wreaths and hummingbirds caught in flight, but now all those sharp clean-edged images were smoothed down, polished with age or use. Inside it, the driver and the fruit girl awaited her patiently, curled up together like a single new fern. The doors opened and out they stepped – arm in arm! – into the moonlight, its shifting registers and difficult qualia. They were an aquatint; simultaneously they were the inevitable early-Cubist shattering of the visible. They didn't seem to notice how unusual everything was.

'I'm not happy with this,' Marnie said to the driver.

By now she could be sure it was, if not Phillip, then a version of him, a bad guess, an attempt tailored to her needs, her own sentimentalised memory.

'You couldn't ever be him!' she said. All this was something being forced on her, she felt, rather than just the pantomime of entities that had no idea how to be human. The room was suddenly full of projections. It was full of counter-transference.

'I can have another name. If you like,' the driver offered.

'He can have another name,' the girl repeated, carefully closing the door of the armoire. 'Just for you!'

'He's not a he. He's an it and so are you. Another thing: why have I been so ill?'

The fruit girl laughed. 'You are pregnant, I guess!'

'Don't be stupid. I'm seventy years old.'

'You are pregnant with Phillip. You are so pregnant!'

The girl threw up her arms and proceeded to dance about the room, skipping and pirouetting and kicking up her heels. Lacing her fingers across her chest and sticking out her elbows, she began bobbing and rocking jauntily side to side from the hips, then, half raising, half spreading her arms and flapping her hands loosely at the wrist, she sang: 'Your beautiful boy Phillip!' Her face was as big as an adult's now, her round cheeks the shine and colour of Turing's apple, the shape of the cheeks of the wind in the corner of an old ocean chart. Then, indicating the driver:

'This is your Phillip. You can have him now!'

The room had darkened with the coming storm. The sound of the tractor stopped at last. Thunderclouds closed in over the woods and the little field. In the flashes of lightning, Marnie clutched her tote. A great calm, a hypnotic calm, came over her. There was a loud noise. Later, all she would remember was glimpsing her own shadow on the wall. It was huge. It was heavily delineated. She watched it lean across the shadow of the driver, which yearned and stretched up to meet it. Her shadow was extending its lower jaw like a drawer sliding open.

'Eat your Phillip now!' the girl was urging. 'Yum!'

The unreliability of the received

—

AFTER SHE HAD SHOT THEM, she put on her old coat, picked up her bag and let herself out quietly, and went down to the beach to watch the old men, working their way back down from 28,000 feet from their nightly raids on Dresden and Agincourt, coming home to roost curled up invisibly between the slats of the memorial benches and in corners of the lofts of the abandoned beachfront houses, where all their guilt at never having been in a war could be quietly and usefully sublimed into the faint smells of balsa glue and butyrate dope, the bales of *Warlord*, *Boys' World* and *Commando* secured like love letters with coloured string.

The storm had passed. The tide was full but the sea was calm; the air was still. She wasn't sure she had killed the girl. It had been such a moment of confusion, so quick yet so endlessly stretched out. A slow pan of the mayhem in the room would perhaps reveal a trail of fluids, the fruit girl absent, the wardrobe doors hanging open again. Below the surface of the water, Marnie felt the driver's many helpers wriggle playfully between her legs, darting away then back again in a kind of comic panic, like children pretending to flee a beloved authority figure. They would miss the stability of that, she thought. She waded a yard or two further in, took out the Hampson diary, read at random: 'By now it was two in the morning. The fireworks had finished long ago. I ran some comparisons with older data, to see if I had received anything like it before. Nothing. Poor reception is only part of the problem. The rest is the unreadability of the information. Afterwards I sat in the kitchen, drinking tea and listening. The aerial was making sounds loud enough to be heard over the wind. I wondered if I should go up to the outbuilding where I kept it, then decided not to. It would need replacing soon anyway. I went to bed instead.'

Unable to make anything of it, she threw both diary and pistol into the sea, returned to the Auberge St Edward, and over the next two days, ate parts of the artefact, slicing it as thinly as she could. After that, though she had never learned how to drive, she found that it came easily to her. She left early on the third day and kept going north along the coast, driving carefully but with increasing confidence. The rooms she stayed in during her journey were often full of a strong old-fashioned scent she associated with the barbershops of Deal and Margate – although it might equally have been confectionary. It was on the edge between perfume and citrus and also – since there was no one but her in the room – seemed liminal in its actual nature, that is, both there and not there. A little later it was gone.

She would get up and walk about in a restless way, not exactly sniffing the air but holding it in her nose then breathing out slowly, lifting her head like an animal bringing into play an olfactory organ human beings don't have. She kept a geranium in a pot in the back of the car, reached behind her now and then while driving, to crush a leaf.

Eggs!

—

The genius loci of the Auberge St Edward is seen bending stiffly over his little tractor. He's tuning this; he's tweaking that. He's banging it with the heel of his hand. He's making adjustments. We watch with interest as large volumes of white smoke are released to drift slowly across the field and into the woods where they break up and wind ropily between the trees. This process the old man regards with a strange combination of satisfaction and detachment. Everything, he thinks, is process. Days have passed. He's home from a difficult job in another part of the country. He limps up and down the dry furrows – stopping to stare with approval into one of the wilder upper corners of his field, as if he has heard something new among the brambles – then enters the auberge via one of its many accessible back doors. The tractor meanwhile sits unattended where the smoke is thickest and musingly explores its own power curve. Eventually the old man re-emerges via a different door and holding out at arm's length a fetid ball of rags. Soon he's dabbing at this; he's dabbing at that. No change. The engine continues to run. The amount of smoke generated, its chemical edge in the nose and earthy overtones on the palate, have a real power to astonish. The old man dodges into it. He dodges out. Bend down, dart in and out, dart in and out, round and round, round again, dab at the engine from a distance, dab from close up: to the eye of a viewer – someone pressed close, for instance, against the glass of an upstairs window of the auberge, distanced by the height and angle – this might resemble a dance. But in all honesty, the old man is too stiff and too slow and too bow-legged for it to be that, and by now the rags are smoking too. We note his nose and eyes; they are running copiously. We note how he employs the smoking rags to wipe the strings of mucus from his cheeks and chin, then, with a fierce cry, mounts the tractor and, elbows and knees out at angles, addresses himself to the churned earth again with the rusty plough, leaving behind tormented, scraped-looking surfaces across which his dog must follow gingerly, as over hot embers. Once the job is finished, if it ever can be said to be either begun or finished, he'll switch off the tractor and abandon it where it stands, canted a little across the careful furrows so it faces towards the woods. The smoke will thin. It will drift away. The old man will stretch his legs, stand straight and stop shaking. He'll blow his nose one more time on the rags, then throw them down. He'll gently encourage the dog, using its name. He'll squat and scrabble in the earth until he's uncovered a row of polished oval stones. 'These here,' he'll tease, 'are eggs! Eggs!' and hurl a stone across the field and watch the dog run. The dog's a new acquisition for him. He likes it. He's taken to a dog before, and kept it, but this one came out of the woods one day covered in mud and sores and took to him and kept him. Once he's teased it enough, he'll go back through the house, down a hall, out of the front door and under the contemporary scaffolding, in a single fluid, swooping movement, a trajectory of intent so full of confidence and energy it can end only at the bar of the Auberge St Edward where – when he isn't working elsewhere, on behalf of others – he has spent much of every day for much of his seventy years; where he and his friends will soon be chuckling about some prank of his when they were young.

The fruit girl and the driver look on. Then the fruit girl turns away from the window and she says:

It's always late afternoon in here.

And then: Look how beautiful I am now.

Are we alive at all? the driver says.

Look out of the glass, she says: You'll see!

They watch the old man for a moment, and something

about his gently inturned certainty, like music, causes them to parade solemnly around the room together, elbows linked, touching each object briefly but lovingly as they pass: the wardrobe, the spilt playing cards like doorways in the afternoon, the spilt and dried fluids and the astral jelly on the floor.

What has happened here? It's as if they have learned to speak but not what it's for. They learn fast. They are not dead. Mornings, the driver sits with its feet in a bucket half filled with water and its shoulders in the sunlight from the window, asking her about the things it can see. Evenings, the fruit girl will often leave it to its own devices while she slips from bar to bar along the seafront. It's love. It's love like the old man's love for his new dog, close yet distant. It is as if you can want everything – for everyone, on behalf of every living thing – yet remain at a distance of care. This is how the tide offers its objects to the beach, the fruit girl says, and how the beach accepts them. This is how we go between the planes. This is how we slip into their world. Don't you remember? It's a kind of dance too.

The driver says: We didn't find what we expected!

It says: I don't remember who I am, I only remember who I am now!

I'm not complete, it says, and they laugh.

And yet you will be! You will be complete. Look, eat this fruit. And this one, they are *so full of vitamins.* The old man plants them so they come up! You'll be complete again soon!

We see that everything she offers the driver is votive – something votive but a joke too. She looks at herself in the mirror, she catches her own smell. *Now* we're on the Good Ship Lollipop, she says. And what it is to be alive, the way they are. This is what it's been about all along.

Scattering the ashes

—

MARNIE CONTINUED TO DRIVE NORTH, stopping for lunch in one place, petrol the next. Then she turned inland. In the car with her she had her collection of constructivist cycle jerseys she had retrieved from the art museum. Some crayons. Two versions of the lost continent sign she felt were worth keeping. Her cotton tote, a little cleaner than usual, its slogan more readable: FILBA INTERNACIONAL 2019. The gun, obviously, lay at the bottom of the sea. Apart from a single page, carefully torn out and folded, Hampson's diary was down there with it. She felt they deserved to be together.

She always kept the biscuit box on the front seat beside her, so that Phillip became a helpless passenger in his own car, stopping only to open it on a different hill or prominence every day. She shook out a handful of him into the wind at each site. You can love all you want, she told herself. Possess the world. Allow it to possess you. There are no returns from this strategy, except what's immediate: the light will often fall interestingly on the sea, for instance, and you've been lucky with that. But some other things will never happen. One thing she had observed was that an onshore wind will cheerfully waft back the ashes, as if fetching you something you dropped. Finally, she came to rest on a hill and parked up overlooking the London Basin.

The city lay quiet, not far beneath her in terms of actual altitude, but further than you would think in the way it seemed to offer itself – part map, part drawing, a hybrid presentation bathed in westering light – opening the estuary away to the right like beaten lead, and in the distance, straight in front, depicting the North Downs as a line of indistinct sensual curves. Nothing down there looked entirely real. Sunlight flickered off a thousand windows continually opening and shutting in the new builds of Rotherhithe and the Bermondsey Shore. The older housing crept in its slow Edwardian way up and down the hilly streets of Peckham and Clapham, while the oldest huddled in its traditional enclaves and warrens. Attack helicopters clattered to and fro, while above it all, the obsolete bombers in their holding patterns dipped clean grey and white wings lazily over Barnes and Richmond, queuing for the turn towards the financial sector, wayfinding by the iconic stumps of the Shard and Undershaft – London's own

Twin Towers – where they would flatten off and light up the afterburners for their final approach to the financial quarter. How Phillip had loved them as a boy!

Looking north, she made out a single vast procession of the iGhetti, towering above the houses of Catford, Lewisham and Blackheath, moving east towards the sea – sometimes like the pure white plumes of a phosphorous explosion, sometimes like great glittering chandeliers. Dim mechanical noises came up now and then; a smell like indoor fireworks and ice cream. No one knew what they were doing down there. People said the sounds they made were horrible, but from Marnie's vantage by the car park ticket machine, all you could hear was something that resembled harmonium music: faint, dronelike, full of resonance, breaking now and then into glory. There was such a calmness in all this. Things had gone wrong long before they came, and it was possible to admit that now. While she waited for something else to happen (nothing did), she thought about the page of Hampson's diary she had saved. It contained only a single thought –

'Summer. I stood in a long shallow chalk valley half a mile from the sea, listening to the sound of the waves – the sound waves! – amplified by acoustic lensing conditions in the absolutely still air, and came to the inescapable conclusion: the iGhetti are only a mirage. We wait for them to reveal themselves, forgetting what has revealed itself daily since they came. They did not arrive *from* the astral plane: they arrived by reconfiguring it. They are only a refraction of something else in the universe, something we can't know about because it's the other side of some horizon. Perhaps we are too.'

She thought about that. She thought about Phillip, and the girl he had brought down the coast with him. I didn't take to her, she thought. That's for certain. She was out of the car by then, licking the last of his ashes off the upturned palm of her hand before the wind could blow them away, blinking in the sunshine and thinking: any day now. At least life had left her with two molars that matched up. So I can still eat, she thought, as long as I'm careful. And what more can you ask? Then, imagining for just a moment that she had heard the lost dog Andrew again, she pushed through a fringe of urine-smelling undergrowth and found her way up into the woods behind the car park. There was no dog.

'Andrew!' she shouted. 'Andrew! Andrew, I won't call for you again if you don't answer!', and spent a few minutes scraping a hole in the soft black earth to bury Phillip's biscuit tin.

'You and I,' he had once written to her, 'go over the past too much.' And she had written back, 'You should never say that.' If nothing else, it made the past seem like a stationary train, accessible from the platform of the present, as if you could choose which carriage to enter. 'Phillip, nothing in memory ever made itself so available.' What would she remember about him in the end anyway that could be separated from everything else that happened? Eventually she returned to the car park and got back in the car and drove it down into the city.